CHRONICLES OF THE MOON

LEGEND OF THE GOLDEN ELEPHANT

CHRONICLES OF THE MOON

LEGEND OF THE GOLDEN ELEPHANT

by Allan Frewin Jones

APPLE SERIES

SCHOLASTIC INC.

New York   Toronto   London   Auckland   Sydney
Mexico City   New Delhi   Hong Kong   Buenos Aires

For Benjamin Neal Oliver, with love and magic

ISBN 0-439-85671-X

Text copyright © 2006 by Working Partners Limited
Created by Ben M. Baglio
Cover illustrations copyright © 2006 by Ed Gazsi

12 11 10 9 8 7 6 5 4 3 2 1   6 7 8 9 10 11/0

Printed in the U.S.A.
First Scholastic printing, October 2006

40

Chapter One: 🌙
A Dramatic Encounter

Josh Welles huddled in the doorway, clinging tightly to its frame as the deck of the riverboat rocked and swayed under him. The vessel was gathering speed as it sailed on down the river. Josh knew there was no one on the bridge. The captain was fighting alongside his few remaining crew members for control of the vessel. Josh heard gunfire from on deck as the attackers advanced on the captain's position. He noticed that a fire had broken out in the stern — red flames and billowing black smoke rose high into the clear blue sky.

He looked around frantically for his friend, Olly Christie. Everywhere, passengers cowered behind chairs, under tables, and in stairwells as bullets tore overhead. He spotted Olly crouched beneath the stairs leading to the upper deck, not far from him.

Suddenly, there was an explosion below deck and the whole boat shuddered. The iron stairs above Olly were wrenched from their fixings in two places. They creaked and groaned, listing ominously.

"Olly!" Josh called. "Get out of there! Fast!"

Olly nodded and ran to the shelter of the open doorway.

Josh could see a few men wearing crew uniforms still fighting back — but it was a very one-sided battle. Most had already been defeated — some looked as if they were dead, others wounded. A fight erupted on an upper deck as three crewmen sprang on one of the gunmen. They wrestled his gun from him, but in the struggle he lurched backward over the rail and fell — a long scream trailing behind him. Machine-gunfire rattled from above. There were more screams. Another explosion.

This mayhem had erupted in just a few minutes. Before the first shots had rung out, Josh and Olly had been lounging on the deck of the passenger cruiser, basking in the sunshine and watching the beautiful scenery of the forested north Indian valley slip slowly past. Then the gang of armed men had moved into action.

"Agent Jack Kelly! Show yourself or we will kill her!" shouted a voice above the noise of the battle.

Josh peered out along the foredeck from his hiding place. He saw his mother. She was being held hostage. Josh could also see the agent the gunman was calling to. He was crouched behind the rail on the upper deck. Josh watched breathlessly as he drew a pistol from his shoulder holster and leaped over the rail.

Then a terrified voice screamed from the prow, "We're heading for Elephant Falls!"

Olly and Josh ran to the rail and leaned over the side of the boat to peer ahead. Sure enough, the boat had traveled well past the jetty where it should have docked. Now it was speeding toward Elephant Falls, where the rushing torrent of the river plunged into a haze of sunlit mist. A rainbow arched through the rising clouds of vapor, and the water shined like silver as it tumbled over the lip of a mighty waterfall and plummeted ninety feet down a rugged cliff face.

It was so close, Josh thought. Surely nothing could stop the boat from plunging over the waterfall. They would all be smashed to pieces on the rocks below.

〰〰〰

"Cut!" The amplified voice rose above the noise.

Olly and Josh were almost jolted off their feet as the boat was brought to an abrupt halt by powerful steel cables anchored to the riverbank. The gunfire stopped. The dead men got up. And the terrified-looking passengers relaxed as cameras ceased rolling.

Several stunt coordinators ran forward with extinguishers to put out the flames.

The actor playing the part of Jack Kelly had landed on a large, inflated plastic mattress. He clambered off, grinning and waving to general applause.

"That was great, Ben," cried the film director. "Thanks everyone — good work. That's a wrap for today."

Olly and Josh ran over to join the glamorous Natasha Welles, who was standing chatting to her kidnappers and to her handsome costar, Ben Wilder.

"So — how do you two like being in the movies?" Natasha asked, smiling at her twelve-year-old son and his best friend.

"It's cool!" Olly replied. She looked at Ben. "Do you think they'd let me do one of those neat dives onto the mattress?" she asked. "It looked fun!"

"You'll have to check that with Giovanni," he said. Giovanni Bosconi was the director of *Collision Course*, a multimillion-dollar, continent-hopping action thriller.

"Hey," Ben continued, pulling a small writing pad out of his jacket pocket. "I've been meaning to ask — could I have your autographs?"

Olly and Josh stared at him.

"Excuse me?" Josh said. "*You* want *our* autographs?"

Natasha laughed. "Didn't I tell you?" she said. "Ben is a big fan of yours."

"I'm really into archaeology," Ben explained. "Natasha's told me how you and Olly's father have been traveling the world, hunting for the lost Talismans of the Moon. And you two were right there when three of the talismans were found!" He pushed the pad and pen into Olly's hands. "That's why I want your autographs. It has nothing to do with your future film careers."

Olly grinned as she signed and handed the book to Josh. The two friends had been a big part of Professor Christie's search for the ancient talismans. "Do you think someone might make a movie about the search for the talismans?" she asked.

"It would certainly make a great story," Natasha said. "Just think of the exotic locations — a tomb in the Valley of the Kings in Egypt, a lost city in a volcano in China, a temple in the Bolivian rain forest . . ."

"And now the Mandakin Valley in Uttaranchal in India," Olly finished, her eyes shining with excitement as she gazed around the rolling, green country at the base of the foothills of the mighty Himalayan Mountains.

"So, tell me, which talisman is the professor looking for now?" Ben asked.

"The Elephant of Parvati," Josh told him. "The legend says that it's a small statuette of an elephant, made of solid gold and covered with diamonds and rubies and emeralds and sapphires! But it wasn't Professor Christie's idea to search for it in the Mandakin Valley," he continued. "We're here because of an ancient parchment that was found close by a few weeks ago."

"Only a few people have seen it so far, and none of them can translate it," Olly added. "There's going to be a big conference at the Peshwar Palace, starting tomorrow — all the top archaeologists in the world will be there." She sighed. "Of course, the discussions won't really get going till Dad arrives since he is an expert on the Talismans of the Moon. He's been held up in Oxford with some boring college business, but he'll be here in a day or two. That's when things will really take off."

Natasha smiled at Ben. "Olly's very proud of her father, as you can tell," she said. "And with good reason, but Ethan has played an important part as well. It was one of Ethan's researchers who discovered the parchment in the first place, and it's Ethan who's organized the conference at the Peshwar Palace."

Olly and Josh exchanged a private look. What Josh's mother said was quite true — her American boyfriend, Ethan Cain, had organized the conference and was footing the bill for the expedition to find the fourth Talisman of the Moon. But they would both have preferred it if he was not involved at all.

Olly and Josh had good reason to dislike the American millionaire. They had seen a side of him that he had managed to hide from most people. Ever since Professor Christie had started his search for the four fabled Talismans of the Moon, Ethan Cain had been somewhere in the background — desperate to get to the talismans first. He was ruthless and cunning and perfectly prepared to use criminal means to get his way — but the worst of it was that Josh and Olly had absolutely no proof of his underhand dealings. Without hard evidence, no one would believe that the good-looking and charming businessman wasn't just as he appeared: an enthusiastic fan of archaeology. But Olly and Josh were sure Ethan was as selfish as he seemed. And this time, he was in complete control of the expedition to find the final talisman known as the Elephant of Parvati.

It wasn't simply because the Talismans of the Moon were of immense archaeological value that they had attracted so much attention; there was also a legend attached to them. It was said that if all the talismans could be gathered together, then they would reveal a great secret. It was Olly and Josh's belief that Ethan Cain wanted to learn that secret and use it for his own purposes.

"But what I don't get is why Ethan won't let anyone see the parchment before the conference starts," Olly said.

"He's invested a lot of time and money in this project," Natasha replied. "He has to keep control of the information, otherwise people could take advantage of him." She shook her head and laughed. "Sometimes, Olly, you almost sound like you're still suspicious of him."

Olly and Josh had tried once before to convince Natasha and the other adults not to trust Ethan — but the millionaire had talked his way out of it, making Olly and Josh look like foolish, overly imaginative children in the process. Olly knew there was no point in starting up that old argument again.

She was still trying to think of a tactful way to respond to Natasha's comment when there was a shuddering bump. The riverboat had returned to the dock. Olly was happy for the distraction.

"OK, people," called Giovanni Bosconi. "Please make your way safely off the boat. We'll be doing some pick-up shots tomorrow, so I want everyone involved to be ready by seven o'clock in the morning. And please remember that we're relocating to the Temple of Ganesha the following day. We only have access to the temple for the one day, so I need everyone to be on their toes."

Olly, Josh, Natasha, and Ben joined the stream of people disembarking. Crowded all around the dock were trailers, trucks, and jeeps, carrying all the cumbersome equipment and supplies needed for shooting such a big-budget film on location.

The assistant director met Ben as they walked off the jetty, talking at high speed about interviews and TV promo appearances as she led him away. Ben smiled at them over his shoulder and gave a helpless shrug.

Josh's twenty-one-year-old brother, Jonathan, was waiting for them at Natasha's trailer, sitting on the steps that led up to the door. Jonathan was Professor Christie's assistant — and a brilliant archaeological student in his own right. But since

Professor Christie was still in England, Jonathan had some time off.

He smiled as they approached. "How did it go?" he asked. "Did everything explode in the right places?"

"It was awesome!" Olly replied. "I'm expecting an Oscar nomination for 'Best Frightened Extra.'"

"It went very well," Natasha said, her arms resting around Olly's and Josh's shoulders. "And these two were great."

Jonathan laughed. "So — are you two planning a career in the movies now? Do you think you could handle being international celebrities?"

"It would be great to be rich and famous," Olly confessed, "but I still think I'd rather be an archaeologist, like Dad. Helping him find the rest of the talismans is much more important to me than being on the cover of *People*."

"I don't see why you two can't be glamorous celebrities *and* legendary archaeologists," Natasha said with a laugh.

"That would be great," Olly said thoughtfully. "But if I had to choose, I'd be an archaeologist."

Josh grinned. "That's so she can finally get rid of the creepy Christie family curse," he said.

Natasha looked interested. "You don't believe in the curse, do you, Olly?"

Olly frowned. "Well, to be honest, I don't really know," she explained. "But the parchment that William Christie, my great-great-grandfather, took from that tomb in Egypt said that the firstborn son in each generation would die young — and so far that's exactly what's happened! William's oldest son died. And then Great-uncle Adam — who was the firstborn son of William's *second* son — died in a shipwreck while he was trying to take the parchment back to the tomb. And then, most recently, Dad's older brother died young, too — in a car crash in 1964."

"But your father is a scientist," Natasha pointed out. "Surely he can't believe in curses?"

"He says not," Olly agreed. "But he first got interested in archaeology while he was researching stuff about the curse." She shrugged. "And you never know. It is odd that they all died."

"Those family deaths are just coincidences," Jonathan said reassuringly. "Don't worry, there are no such things as curses."

Olly looked at him. The sensible part of her knew he had to be right — but there was another part of her that wasn't so sure. And the thing that sometimes worried her was the uncomfortable knowledge that, for the first time since William Christie had removed the cursed writings from the ancient tomb, there was no firstborn son to suffer the Christie curse. Olly was an only child — her mother had died in a tragic plane crash two years previously. And there were no other kids in her generation.

If there really was a curse, and if there was no firstborn son, Olly wondered what would happen. Would the curse die out, or would it come down on her instead?

It wasn't a very pleasant thought.

Chapter Two: ☾
The Peshwar Palace

Jonathan was at the wheel of a rented jeep as it bounced its way down the unpaved road that led to the Peshwar Palace, some six or seven miles below Elephant Falls. Josh was beside him and Olly was in the back, kneeling on the seat and looking back the way they had come — staring into the far, far distance where the jagged, snowcapped peaks of the Himalayas reached up to the sky in a misty blue haze.

Closer, but still many miles away, the rumpled brown mountains of northern Uttaranchal gathered in crags and ravines. The nearer mountains became greener and greener as they tumbled down into forested foothills and lush river valleys.

Olly could see how this astounding place had caught Natasha's eye when she and Ethan had first flown over it in his helicopter. Natasha had suggested it to the producers of *Collision Course* as an excellent location for a dramatic action sequence — and within weeks the whole crew had been sent here.

The filming of the hijacked riverboat had taken place on a wide stretch of the Nintal River, as it flowed through the Mandakin Valley. To the north, the Nintal wound its way between steep valley walls, where pilgrim trails led to remote temples deep in cedar forests.

The jeep bounced and jolted as Jonathan carefully steered it along the path that snaked back and forth down the steep cliffs bordering Elephant Falls. They had reached the point where the trail came closest to the falls. Here, the road took a hairpin turn on a shelf of black rock that was permanently wet with spray. Jonathan brought the jeep to a halt and the three of them gazed in wonder at the curtain of white water that cascaded over the thirty-yard fall of the cliff face.

Olly rolled down the window, leaning out to feel the spray on her face and to hear the roar of the rushing water. "It's amazing!" she shouted over the thunder of the waterfall.

She had seen many wonderful and astonishing sights in her travels with her father, but the power and beauty of Elephant Falls took her breath away.

Down below, the falls flowed into one end of a long, oval-shaped lake. At the far end of the lake, the river flowed on, channeled by rocky banks into a long stretch of stony white water that tumbled away out of sight around a shoulder of the hills.

"I love this place!" Olly shouted, her heart pounding. "Oh, look!" she yelled, leaning out even farther and pointing to something even more wonderous on the far shore of the lake. "Elephants!"

Olly counted five full-grown elephants, as well as three calves, walking with slow majesty toward the crystal water of the lake. There were half a dozen men with them, two seated high on the backs of the lead elephants, the others walking alongside.

"There's an elephant orphanage over there," Jonathan said, pointing to the east. "There's a real problem with poachers in this region. They'll kill anything that will make them a quick profit — elephants, rhinos, tigers — you name it. So they have a shelter for the orphaned animals."

"How could anyone kill an elephant?" Josh wondered aloud, staring down at the huge creatures. "Do you think we could go down there and see them close-up?"

"Not right now, but I don't see why you couldn't come back," Jonathan replied. "It's not too far from the Peshwar Palace, but you'd have to watch out for the monkeys. I'm told they're great pickpockets. They'll snatch your things before you know what's happening — especially if you're carrying food."

They watched the elephants for a few minutes, then Jonathan started up the engine and they set off again. The jeep rounded a rocky cliff and then the waterfall, the lake, and the elephants were out of view.

Far ahead in the distance, where things were pale and hazy, the friends could just make out the town of Tauri, where the cast and crew of *Collision Course* were staying. But their destination was much closer at hand. Nestled in a small valley less than a mile ahead was the beautiful and impressive Peshwar Palace, shining like a jewel among the tall cedar trees.

It was a tall, square building of white stone, its walls punctuated by arched windows and ornate balconies. The high roof was adorned with slender white towers, extravagant domes, and golden minarets that flashed in the sunlight. The palace was surrounded by wide ornamental gardens of green, velvety lawns and flowerbeds blooming with color.

Fifty years ago, the palace had been transformed into a luxury hotel. And it was here that Ethan Cain had arranged for the archaeological elite from around the world to gather and discuss the parchment that he believed would guide them to the priceless Elephant of Parvati.

"The palace was built by the Mughal emperor in 1647," Josh told Olly. "It was supposed to be for his oldest son, but he died young and the emperor's second son, Balaram, inherited it instead. But then he was killed when the Chand Rajahs invaded and took over the country. Lots of different people have dominated this area over the past few hundred years, but the British managed to stop the final invasion in the 1800s."

Olly stared at him. "Josh, you can be kind of weird," she said. "How do you know all that?"

Josh grinned at her. "I looked it up on the Internet last night. Anyone could have done it."

Olly laughed. "Yes, but no one who is normal would have memorized it!"

The mountain path joined a more substantial road as it winded its way down to the hotel. Jonathan brought the jeep to a stop in a gravel parking lot, and then the three of them made their way to the front of the palace and up the broad marble steps to the wide veranda.

Ethan Cain was seated at one of the white, wrought-iron tables near the magnificent archway into the palace. He was working at a laptop, but he stopped and stood up with a smile and a wave, as Jonathan and the two friends came toward him.

"I've just been speaking to Natasha on the phone," he said, smiling from Olly to Josh. "She says the two of you should be looking for high-class Hollywood agents to run your future movie careers."

Olly managed a thin smile. "Far from it," she said. "All we had to do was run around looking scared and then cower in a doorway."

"Stay and have a drink with me," Ethan Cain suggested. "You can tell me all about it." He snapped his fingers and a white-clad waiter appeared from nowhere and hovered silently at his shoulder.

"That'd be nice," Olly said. "But I want to go and check with my grandmother and find out if Dad's been in touch yet. I expect you're anxious for him to arrive — I mean, you can't really start the conference without him."

Ethan Cain smiled at her. "Of course. We desperately need your father's expertise, Olly," he said smoothly. "But I really can't keep all these important people waiting around, you know. It wouldn't be fair to them."

Olly frowned. "You mean you *are* going to start without him?"

"I think we can manage a few preliminary discussions before your father arrives," Ethan replied. He looked at Jonathan. "I believe you will be acting as Professor Christie's stand-in until he gets here?"

Jonathan nodded. "That's right," he said. "And I'd like to have a quick word with you about that, if I may."

"Of course." Ethan looked at Olly and Josh. "I think we'll have our first full meeting tomorrow morning," he declared. He lifted a tall glass from the table. "Here's to a successful outcome. Here's to us finding the Elephant of Parvati!"

Olly and Josh exchanged an anxious look. Olly certainly wanted the talisman to be found — but not by Ethan Cain!

~~~~

The reception area of the Peshwar Palace was very elegant. The high, domed ceiling was decorated with thousands of small mirrors that sparkled like trapped stars. Golden pillars framed the arched doorways, and rich blue draperies were swathed over the white walls. Olly and Josh walked across the dark blue-and-white mosaic floor toward the white marble staircase that swept in a long curve to the upper floors.

"Ethan is such a creep," Olly hissed to Josh as

they headed up to the suite of rooms allocated to the Christie party. "I know what he's up to. He's hoping to get that parchment translated before Dad arrives, so he can find the talisman all by himself."

"But even if he does," Josh pointed out, "he'll only have one of them. The professor is still in control of the other three."

"But if Ethan gets even one of the talismans," Olly responded, "it'll mean he can insist on being involved when the rest are found and they're all brought together so that the big secret can be revealed."

Josh frowned. "I wonder if there really is a big secret," he said thoughtfully. At first they had thought there might be just four talismans, but recent research suggested there could be many more — and they all would have to be found before anyone could discover their true purpose.

Olly shrugged. "Dad thinks so," she answered. "According to what he's read, the secret is the location of the lost Archive of Old — and you know what's supposed to be in there, don't you?"

"Copies of every ancient document that has ever been written," Josh confirmed. "Scrolls and parchments and books that have been lost for thousands of years."

"And remember what Jonathan says," Olly added. "He thinks there might be documents in there that prove human civilization has been around for at least twenty-five thousand years longer than anyone realized."

Josh nodded. "Yes, but your dad doesn't think that's very likely, does he?"

"No," Olly admitted. "But once the Archive of Old is found, we'll all know for certain, won't we?" She looked at Josh. "And I really, really don't want Ethan Cain to be in on it!"

"Neither do I," Josh agreed vehemently. "He's not an archaeologist. He's a fake. And he wouldn't be here if he weren't rich. He bought his way in."

"So, our job is to keep a close watch on him and make sure he doesn't get away with anything," Olly declared.

"Agreed."

~~~~~

There was a small brass plaque on the wall outside the double doors of the suite where Olly and Josh's party was staying.

In these rooms, the eminent archaeologist, Sir Oliver Gordon-Howes, lived and worked during his exploratory expedition to the region in 1903.

"Considering how famous Sir Oliver was, I'm

surprised Ethan didn't want these rooms for himself," Olly said.

"He's taken over the biggest suite of rooms in the whole place," Josh told her. "The Maharajah's Suite. It covers almost the whole top floor."

"He would!" Olly replied. "But I bet it's not as interesting as the rooms he gave us."

She opened the door and they stepped into a large sitting room with many doors leading out of it. The room was almost a museum to Sir Oliver Gordon-Howes.

A bookcase held copies of his published works, and a glass-topped cabinet displayed his diaries, open at pages filled with a pale scrawl and rough drawings. Another tall cabinet held Sir Oliver's compass, an old box camera in a cracked leather case, and the hat from the photos. Alongside these were a few of the artifacts he had discovered: small dancing figures sculpted from black stone; carved images of the elephant-headed god, Ganesha; and a brown pottery elephant with a small, mouselike animal sitting on its curled-up trunk. Olly wondered if these were recreations — or the real thing.

A large, framed map of the region hung on the wall, showing Sir Oliver's travels marked out in red ink. Many more maps, some much older, were kept in a special room on the ground floor of the hotel. Olly and Josh planned to investigate that room as soon as they got the opportunity. In fact, they intended to thoroughly explore the whole palace — it would give them something interesting to do while Jonathan and the others were working on translating the ancient parchment.

"Ahh, here you are." Olly's grandmother stepped in from a side room. Audrey Beckmann was a tall, elegant woman with gray hair cut in a neat bob. Ever since the death of Olly's mother, she had been looking after Olly and her father on their travels. When Natasha Welles's lifestyle had proved too erratic to provide her younger son with a stable home life, Josh had joined his brother and the Christies. Now Mrs. Beckmann was tutor to both Olly and Josh. As an ex-teacher, she was, in Olly's opinion, just a little too intense when it came to schoolwork. She insisted on lessons every weekday morning, even when there were far more exciting things to do.

"Josh and I have decided we're going to run away and be movie stars," Olly joked. "If that's OK with you, Gran."

Mrs. Beckmann raised an eyebrow. "I take it you enjoyed yourselves today, then," she said.

Olly grinned widely. "It was great!" she replied. "There were people firing guns, and bombs going off all over the place, and Ben did this amazing leap off the top deck."

"Good, then I'll look forward to a five-hundred-word essay on it as your homework assignment," Mrs. Beckmann said firmly. "That will make up for you both missing lessons this morning."

Olly sighed but she knew better than to argue the point. "I don't suppose you've heard from Dad, have you?" she asked.

"As a matter of fact, I have," Mrs. Beckmann told her. "I spoke to him on the telephone about an hour ago."

"When's he coming?" Olly asked eagerly. "He'd better get here soon. Ethan's planning on having the first meeting tomorrow."

"According to your father, his work in Oxford should be finished the day after tomorrow," her grandmother said. "And he's going to take the first flight he can. So we can expect him here in three days' time."

Olly smiled. "That's great," she sighed, relieved. "They're never going to be able to figure out what the parchment says that quickly."

"I wouldn't be too sure about that," Jonathan

said as he came through the door. "There are going to be some real experts around the conference table tomorrow morning."

"Not as expert as Dad," Olly said confidently.

Jonathan laughed. "We'll see."

"You're so lucky," Josh said gloomily. "I'd really like to be in there with you."

Jonathan smiled. "Oh, didn't I mention it?" he teased. "I asked Ethan if it would be OK for the two of you to attend some of the talks — and he said yes. So he's going to set out two chairs for you at the table tomorrow morning. As long as your grandmother approves, of course."

Olly and Josh both looked eagerly at Mrs. Beckmann.

"I think that would be a very good idea," she responded.

Olly grinned. This was great! Now, Ethan Cain wouldn't be able to get up to anything underhanded in her father's absence, at least not without her and Josh knowing all about it.

Chapter Three: ☾
The Whispering Shrew

It was quarter to ten the following morning. The first meeting of the International Conference on the Uttaranchal Parchment was due to begin in a quarter of an hour. Josh sat at the table in the main room of their hotel suite. Mrs. Beckmann had insisted that he and Olly wear their nicest clothes. They were waiting for Jonathan to take them down to the conference room.

Olly stood on the balcony, which provided a wonderful view of the beautiful palace gardens with their fragrant lilies, roses, and other exotic flowers. Slender, juniper-lined walkways led to sheltered arbors and to fountains and pools of still, clear water where golden carp swam. Beyond the gardens, the valley rose up into green hills and distant mountains.

Jonathan rushed from room to room, assembling his papers and pausing in front of the mirror every now and then to adjust his tie or smooth his hair.

Josh watched his brother in amusement — it

wasn't often that Jonathan showed signs of nerves, but he was clearly anxious about the conference meeting.

Mrs. Beckmann handed notepads and pens to Josh and Olly. "I want you to make notes of the meeting," she told them. "And I'd like you to write them up as minutes — you know what minutes are, don't you?"

"Of course," Olly sighed. "Minutes are a record of everything that happens."

Mrs. Beckmann nodded. "Now listen, both of you," she said. "You are very privileged to be allowed into this meeting — I want you to promise to behave yourselves."

Olly gave her an affronted look. "What's that supposed to mean?" she asked.

"I think it means that your grandmother doesn't want you telling them that they won't be able to translate the parchment without the professor," Josh said with a grin.

"That's exactly what I mean," said Mrs. Beckmann. "I want you both on your very best behavior. This will be a marvelous learning experience for you, so — mouths shut, Olly, and ears open wide."

"Why are you picking on me?" Olly demanded.

"I wonder," Mrs. Beckmann said with a half smile.

Jonathan joined them, a stack of documents under one arm, and his laptop under the other. "OK," he said, slightly breathlessly. "Is everyone ready?"

"We've been ready for half an hour," Olly pointed out.

"Then let's go."

Soon they were walking quickly down the magnificent corridors of the palace toward the tall double doors of the conference room.

Inside, they found a handful of people were already there, some going through papers, others standing and talking quietly together beside the polished, dark-wood table. On the wall at one end of the room hung a large screen, and Josh spotted a projector at the far end of the table.

A small, gray-haired Asian man walked up to them. "You are Mr. Welles, Professor Christie's assistant?" he asked Jonathan.

"Yes, Professor Wu," Jonathan replied. "And this is my brother, Josh, and Professor Christie's daughter, Olivia."

The professor bowed his head politely toward

the two friends. Josh had seen pictures of Professor Wu in his brother's archaeological magazines — he was China's foremost expert in ancient languages.

"If I may, I would like a word about Professor Christie's thoughts so far," Professor Wu said. He pulled Jonathan aside, leaving Olly and Josh standing on their own.

"I know him," Olly said softly, pointing discreetly at a large bearded man. "He's Professor Rostapov. He works in Moscow. And the woman talking to him is Doctor Johansdottir from Iceland. And that thin woman with the long hair is Judith Marx — she's from Berkeley University in California."

They stepped aside as more people entered.

Josh recognized the Nigerian Professor, Mpele, and Doctor McKenzie from Australia. He really did not know *that* many archaeologists by name and face, but it seemed all the ones that he would recognize were there.

"I don't know how Ethan managed to get all these people together in one place!" Olly whispered. "Some of them are really serious rivals. I remember my dad saying that Judith Marx and Doctor McKenzie can't stand the sight of each other. And there are plenty of others here who are always disagreeing with one another in print."

"I suppose Ethan thought it made sense to invite people with different opinions," Josh said.

"He's certainly done that," Olly replied. She gazed around the room as more renowned people came in. "This is going to be amazing. I can't wait to hear what they all have to say about the parchment."

"Good morning, Josh and Olly," came Ethan Cain's voice from close behind them.

They turned to see Ethan with a young man who he introduced as his assistant, Paul White. Paul smiled. He was slightly shorter than Ethan and looked immaculate in a tailored suit. He was clutching a briefcase.

Ethan rested a hand briefly on Olly's shoulder. "This should be interesting — plenty of lively debate, I should think. It's such a pity your father can't be here when we kick things off."

"We're expecting him in a couple of days," Olly told him.

"Really? That's great. I'm looking forward to it." He smiled. "Now, I think I should get this show on the road." He swept past the friends, closely followed by Paul.

Olly stared after Ethan as he greeted the gathered archaeologists. "I've got my eye on you," she murmured under her breath.

A couple of minutes later, Ethan brought the meeting to order. Everyone found their seats and the murmur of voices faded to an expectant silence.

Paul White laid the briefcase on the table and opened it. He took out a sheaf of brown folders and began to move quietly around the table, placing one in front of each person present — including Josh and Olly. Once he had finished, he closed the briefcase and quietly left the room.

Ethan Cain stood up. He gazed slowly around the table, and Josh saw a look of quiet triumph cross his face. The businessman was clearly reveling in the moment. *He must be in his element*, Olly thought, *being at the head of this big boardroom table*.

"I'd like to start by welcoming you all to the Peshwar Palace and thanking you for making time in your busy schedules to attend this meeting. As you are probably all aware, Kenneth Christie will not be able to join us for a couple of days, but in his place I would like you to welcome his very able assistant, Jonathan Welles, the son of my good friend Natasha Welles, the actress." He smiled. "I hope our endeavors will prove less arduous than the film that is currently being shot near here." There was a low ripple of polite laughter. "Seated with Mr. Welles are his brother, Josh, and Professor Christie's daughter, Olivia." All eyes turned to them. "Olivia, Josh, and I are old friends, and I am especially pleased to have them with us today."

Josh looked carefully into Ethan's eyes, but there was no sign that he didn't mean every word. Whatever dark thoughts he might harbor toward Josh and Olly, he kept them well hidden.

Ethan pressed some buttons on the projector, and a picture appeared on the screen at his back. It was a beautifully colored painting of a richly dressed couple. The man had a pale blue face and a golden crown. The woman's face was rose-pink and she wore an elaborate headdress. Between them, they held a baby, normal in every way but for one thing — it had the head of an elephant.

"This is the Hindu god, Shiva, with his bride, Parvati, and their child, Ganesha," Ethan Cain said. "Legend has it that Shiva did not realize the child was his own, and in a rage, cut its head off. When he learned his mistake, he replaced the lost head with that of an elephant." A second picture appeared. The human with the elephant head again — this time as an adult, with a round belly and four arms. "The child became Ganesha — the god of wisdom and learning — the remover of obstacles," Ethan continued. "You see him here depicted in his usual form, with one broken tusk, and with a discus, a club, a conch shell, and a water lily in his hands."

Another picture appeared behind him — this time it was an enlargement of a cracked and stained parchment, covered with flowing writing.

"This is the parchment that we are here to discuss," Ethan said. "It was discovered by a researcher of mine in an old shrine dedicated to Ganesha in the town of Tauri, about thirty miles south of here. Each of you will find a copy of the parchment in your folders. It is by translating this ancient document that I hope we may discover the resting place of that Talisman of the Moon known as the Elephant of Parvati."

The screen changed to show a drawing of a golden elephant covered in jewels. "The Elephant of Parvati has been lost for millennia," Ethan declared, "but it is said to resemble this artist's rendition."

Josh opened his folder and took out his copy of the parchment. He peered at it. The script was small and fine, consisting of row after row of delicate pen-lines, with loops and curls forming an intricate pattern that hardly looked like writing at all. At the foot of the page was a strange, simple, little illustration: an elephant, with some kind of mouselike animal that was nearly the same size, talking into its ear.

"I would like to pass the floor to Professor Indira Singh, India's foremost authority on ancient scripts," Ethan said.

A tall, slender woman in a bright red sari stood up. "Many of the symbols used in this writing seem similar to an early form of the Devanagari script used in modern Hindi," she said. "But we believe the language is a lost branch of Sanskrit, many thousands of years old. As you will see, it has many similarities to Sanskrit. However, the splitting on the sandhis is quite unlike anything I have encountered before."

Josh had jotted down Sanskrit on his notepad, but now his pen lay still as Professor Singh continued to speak. He had no idea what she was talking about, and when another of the professors interrupted to contradict what she had just said, it suddenly dawned on him that the meeting might not be quite as exciting as he and Olly had hoped.

Olly leaned close to Josh. "Have you got the faintest idea what they're talking about?" she asked.

He shook his head.

Another of the archaeologists joined in the discussion, and soon several people were all trying to speak at the same time. Professor Rostapov pounded his fist on the table to emphasize a point he was trying to make.

Josh could see that Ethan Cain was completely absorbed by the debate. "Ladies and gentlemen," Ethan called, as tempers, and voices, began to rise. "Please! We'll never get anywhere if we all speak at once. Professor Rostapov — I believe you wanted to say something."

"I think we can agree that certain words on this parchment bear a remarkable similarity to the Devanagari words for *full moon* and for *temple*," Professor Rostapov said. "We can therefore deduce that the first section of the writing concerns the Talismans of the Moon." There were murmurs of agreement from various parts of the table. "And the reference to a temple suggests that the talisman may be found in a temple in this region. Now, there is a temple only a few miles from here dedicated to Ganesha — we should surely investigate that before we get bogged down in linguistic detail."

"The Temple of Ganesha has already been thoroughly researched and explored," argued Professor Singh. "Besides which, Professor Rostapov is forgetting that the word preceding *temple* can be translated as *secret* or *hidden* or *missing* — suggesting that the talisman was placed in a temple that was already lost when this parchment was written in the early Harappan Era almost five thousand years ago."

"Surely, if the parchment mentions the moon," Judith Marx broke in, "we should search for a temple linked with the moon."

"I disagree," said Doctor McKenzie. "We need to have a much more thorough understanding of the entire script before we can proceed to search for anything."

A whole new debate erupted at this point. Josh noticed that Olly was slumped in her chair, obviously bored by all the arguing.

Jonathan raised a hand. "Excuse me," he said. "Has anyone given any thought to the illustration at the foot of the page?"

"The elephant and the shrew?" Ethan asked. "Ganesha is very often shown with a shrew companion — I doubt if the picture has any particular relevance to the Elephant of Parvati."

Oh, it's a shrew? Josh thought. *Not a gigantic mouse, then.*

"Yes, but the shrew isn't with Ganesha in this picture," Jonathan persisted. "It's with an ordinary elephant. I'm sure I've seen something similar before with Professor Christie, on a document from the

Vedic Period. It illustrated a part of a story which involved a shrew whispering secrets to an elephant."

"The Vedic Period is too recent to have anything to do with the topic we're discussing, thank you, Jonathan," Ethan said, in a dismissive tone that Josh could tell his brother found quite annoying. Jonathan simply nodded and fell silent.

The debate raged on. Josh was amazed that all these eminent people seemed unable to agree on anything. At this rate, they'd never make any progress. He noticed that the only thing on Olly's pad was a little drawing of a shrew, with a speech bubble over its head in which she had written: *How do you do? I am a shrew.*

He watched as Olly picked up her pencil and scribbled something else on her pad.

This is so unbelievably boring!

Josh looked at the drawing of the shrew. The illustration of the giant shrew and the elephant rang bells in his mind. He'd seen something like it recently — since he'd been at the palace. . . . He sat upright as his memory suddenly clicked into place. He opened his mouth to speak, but closed it again when he saw Ethan Cain's eyes on him from the far end of the table.

He picked up his pen and wrote on Olly's pad,

I remembered something that might be important. Let's go.

Olly looked at him and her eyes widened with interest as she saw his expression. She nodded.

Josh leaned over to his brother. "Is it OK if we leave?" he asked.

"You might as well," Jonathan whispered back. "I think we're going to be bogged down in this argument for some time."

Josh quietly folded up his copy of the parchment and slipped it into his pocket. "We'll see you later," he murmured to his brother. "Have fun."

Jonathan gave him an expressive look.

As quietly as they could, Olly and Josh slipped from their seats and padded to the door. Josh opened it and — just as he was about to close it behind them — he saw that Ethan Cain was staring at them intently.

∿∿∿∿

"I can't believe the way they were arguing back there," Olly said, shaking her head as they made their way up to their hotel suite. "Maybe that explains why a lot of professors and doctors and smart people like that prefer to work on their own." She looked at Josh. "So, what did you remember?"

"You'll see," Josh said.

There was no one in the main room when they got there — Mrs. Beckmann had left a note to say that she had taken a trip into Tauri.

Josh stood in the middle of the room. "OK," he said. "It's in here."

Olly looked at him. "What is?"

"The thing I remembered."

Olly frowned at him. "It's something to do with the parchment, right?"

Josh nodded, grinning.

"OK," Olly said. "If you can figure it out, then so can I." She looked around. "Don't say a word." She walked over to one of the display cabinets and scrutinized the contents.

"Cold," Josh said.

"Shush!" Olly hissed. She moved to another of the cabinets, looked carefully at its contents, and then moved to the next. She stared through the glass top for a few minutes and then smiled. "Got it!"

Josh walked over to join her. Lying on its side in the cabinet — just as he remembered it — was a dark brown pottery elephant, beautifully carved and covered in intricate ornamentation. Its trunk was curved up beside its head, and seated on the trunk, as if whispering into the elephant's ear, was an exquisitely carved little shrew.

"It's like that picture at the bottom of the parchment!" Olly exclaimed. "Except that the elephant and the shrew are the right size here."

"Exactly," Josh said. "A shrew whispering secrets to an elephant — just like Jonathan mentioned."

Olly turned the small gilt handle on the cabinet lid and it swung open. She gave Josh a look of surprise. Why had it not been locked?

"Careful," Josh said as she picked up the pottery elephant. "It looks really old."

"It's heavy," Olly replied.

They walked over to the table and Olly put the elephant down on its four stumpy legs.

"What's that?" Josh asked, pointing to a narrow slit behind the elephant's right ear.

Olly ran her finger along the slit — it was about an inch long and less than half an inch wide. "It's like the slot in a piggy bank," she remarked. "I wonder if there's anything inside." She lifted the elephant and shook it.

"Don't!" Josh said. "If you break it, we'll be in big trouble!"

A faint clattering sounded from inside the elephant.

"There *is* something in there," Olly declared excitedly. She turned the elephant over in her hands, and Josh again heard the sharp clink of something moving about inside. "Do you think it could be money?"

"I don't know," Josh responded. "Is there a hole in the bottom so we can get it out?"

Olly turned the heavy object around, but apart from the slot behind its ear, there was no other break in the pottery.

Josh lifted the elephant out of Olly's hands, turned it upside down, and gently shook it in the hope that the thing inside would fall out.

"That's never going to work," Olly said.

Josh held the elephant up high and tried to peer in through the slot to see what was inside — but the slot was too small and the inside of the elephant was too dark.

"There must be some way of getting it out," Josh said. He looked around. Olly had gone. "Great. Just leave me here talking to myself," he added loudly.

Olly reappeared from her bedroom with a pen-knife.

Josh frowned. "What's that for?" he asked.

"You've never had a piggy bank, have you?" Olly countered with a wide grin.

"No. Why?"

"Give it here and I'll show you," she said.

Josh handed the elephant over. Olly sat cross-legged on the floor with the elephant in her lap. She tilted it sideways and carefully slid the blade of the knife into the slot. Then she leaned sideways, angling the elephant until it was almost upside down.

Josh crouched at her side. "No way," he said doubtfully.

"You'll see."

A few seconds later, something small and slender and silvery slid out of the slot and fell onto the carpet.

Josh picked it up and stared at it. The artifact was clearly very old and he could see that it was engraved with beautiful patterns. But that wasn't what fascinated Josh most: The thing he was holding between his fingers was a tiny, silver key.

Chapter Four: ☾
The Silver Key

Olly and Josh sat at the table. The pottery elephant stood between them, and lying on the tabletop was the delicate, little silver key.

"A treasure chest filled with diamonds and rubies and pearls," Josh said, continuing their game of guessing what the key was for.

"I don't think so," Olly said. "I think it's the key to open the box where the Elephant of Parvati is hidden."

Josh's eyes widened. "Wouldn't that be great?" he said. "Imagine if we could find the box and get to the talisman while all those professors are still arguing about it."

Olly looked at Josh. "But could it really be that simple?" she asked.

Josh shrugged.

The door opened and Jonathan walked in.

"You've finished early," Olly said. "I thought you'd still be arguing for hours."

Jonathan dumped his papers on the table and

slumped into a chair. "So did I," he said, shaking his head. "There are fourteen eminent archaeologists in there — some of the finest minds on the planet — and almost every single one of them has a different idea about what the parchment says and what we should do about it." He ran his fingers through his hair. "We broke early for lunch. Paul came in and said something to Ethan. I don't know what it was, but he adjourned early for lunch. I suppose he must have had a call from California — something to do with his business, no doubt." He looked at the pottery elephant and then from Olly to Josh. "What's this doing out of its case?" he asked. "Do you have any idea how valuable it is?"

Olly placed a finger on the silver key and pushed it across the table toward Jonathan. "Josh remembered seeing the elephant in here when you mentioned that story about a shrew whispering secrets to an elephant."

"We heard a rattling sound when Olly picked it up," Josh added. "There's a little slot. The key was inside."

Jonathan picked up the key and examined it closely. "It's pure silver, I think," he said. "Look at all the fine tracery on it. It must have been made by a master craftsman."

"How old is it?" Olly asked.

"I have no idea," Jonathan replied. He held the key up to the light that streamed in through the French windows. "And here's another fascinating question: Where exactly is the lock that it was made to open?"

There was a knock at the door.

"Come in," Jonathan called.

Ethan Cain appeared in the doorway.

"I just came to check that Olly and Josh weren't too bored by the meeting," he said, smiling as he entered.

Olly stared at him in dismay. Ethan had picked the very worst moment to come to their suite. She reached across the table, desperate to get the key back from Jonathan before Ethan spotted it. But Jonathan turned toward Ethan and the key was shining brightly in his palm.

"I know all that talking can give you a headache," Ethan said. "But I'm afraid that's the price you have to pay for dealing with experts." He came over to the table. "That's attractive," he said, looking down at the key.

Olly prayed that Jonathan wouldn't tell Ethan anything about the key — but it was hopeless.

"Olly and Josh found it inside this pottery

elephant," Jonathan said, gesturing toward the little artifact sitting on the table. "It looks as if it may be quite old."

"Yes, I think it probably is," Ethan said, leaning forward to peer closely at the key.

Olly glanced at Josh. She could see from his face that he was thinking exactly the same thing she was. The very last person they wanted to see the key was Ethan Cain.

"An expert on Indian silverwork should be able to date it from the designs," Ethan said. "We should show it to Professor Singh."

"We were wondering what kind of lock it was made for," Jonathan remarked.

"That's a very good question," Ethan responded. He looked at Olly and there was an amused gleam in his eye. "It might even be the key to where the Elephant of Parvati is hidden," he said. "What do you think, Olly?"

Olly managed to keep her expression neutral. "Could be," she murmured.

"Everyone's in the dining room," Ethan said. "Shall we go and show it to Professor Singh right now? I'm sure we'd all be fascinated by her insights." He held out his hand and Jonathan dropped the key into his palm.

Olly stared in dismay. She couldn't believe that Jonathan had handed the key over so easily. She and Josh watched miserably as the glinting silver key disappeared into Ethan's fist.

~~~~

The dining room was on the ground floor. It opened out onto a wide veranda of white stone that overlooked the palace gardens.

Professor Singh was at a table on the veranda with Professor Marx and the Swedish doctor, Ingmar Froeman.

Ethan placed the key in Professor Singh's hand. "What can you tell us about this, Indira?" he asked.

She looked curiously at the key. "It is of beautiful workmanship," she said. "And very old — I'd say at least two thousand years by the designs engraved on it. It was probably crafted for the lock of a jewelry box or something similar. I have never seen an artifact quite like it. Where did you find it?"

"We found it inside a pottery elephant in our suite," Olly told her. "An elephant with a shrew whispering into its ear — just like on the parchment."

"I think the elephant might date back to the first millennium B.C.," Ethan suggested. "The Mauryan Empire Period, I would estimate. It's too recent for it to have any connection with the talisman, of course, but it is an interesting find."

"It is indeed," Professor Singh agreed. "I would advise you to put this somewhere safe. It is very fragile. Perhaps you could have a copy made. I believe there is a metalworker in the hotel who could do it for you. That way you could search for the lock that fits the key, without any fear that the original key might be damaged."

"That's an excellent idea," Ethan declared. He took the key from her and went in search of the hotel manager.

Olly watched despondently as he took the key away.

"Are you two hungry?" Jonathan asked.

"Not right now," Olly said, trying hard to mask her disappointment that their great find had just disappeared in Ethan's clutches. She looked at Josh. "Do you feel like going for a walk?"

He nodded, looking as fed up as she felt.

They left Jonathan talking with the professors and walked down the wide steps that led to the gardens.

"Leave it to Ethan to show up at exactly the wrong moment," Olly said. "Now we'll never get the chance to find out what that key was for." She sat on the raised marble edge of an ornamental pond. Silver and golden fish glided beneath broad lily pads. "I don't care what they say. I'm sure that key has something to do with the talisman," she said, dabbling her fingers in the cool water.

Josh sat beside her. He pulled out the folded copy of the parchment and smoothed it out on his knees.

Olly stared out across the gardens. A little way off, she saw a friendly face. Salila Gupta was the ten-year-old daughter of the hotel's chef. She had shown Olly and Josh around the palace when they had first arrived, and they had struck up a friendship. Olly loved the clothes that Salila wore: loose tunics and pants of brightly colored cotton, known as salwar kameez.

Olly waved and Salila came over to them. "I am feeding the fish," she explained slowly in clear and carefully pronounced English, showing them a pot of fish food. "It's fun today because they are hungry." She looked at Josh and Olly. "Are you enjoying yourselves at the palace?"

"Not much right now," Olly admitted. "But we'll get over it."

Salila looked at the paper in Josh's lap. "What is that?" she asked.

"It's a copy of an old parchment," he said. "The archaeologists are trying to figure out what it means. Apparently it's in a very old version of Sanskrit — maybe thousands of years old."

"May I see?" Salila asked, sitting down beside him.

Josh gave her the sheet of paper.

"Please tell me you can read it," Olly said with a grin. "That would make our day!"

Salila shook her head. "No," she said. "I cannot read it." Then she looked up at Olly and there was a sparkle in her eyes. "But I know someone who might be able to help."

Josh and Olly gaped at her.

"Are you kidding?" Josh said.

"Excuse me?" Salila asked, her forehead wrinkled.

"He means — are you playing a joke on us?" Olly explained.

"Oh, no, I am not making a joke," Salila replied. "Do you know of the elephant orphanage near here?"

"Yes," Josh told her. "We saw some of the elephants at the lake on our way back from the movie shoot yesterday."

"There is an old mahout there," Salila continued, using the Hindi word for elephant driver. "He is a very wise old man. His family was once rich — they sent him to England to be educated. But when he returned, he gave up all worldly things and chose instead a life of modesty and meditation. His name is Adhita Ram. He is said to be the only man alive now who can speak the ancient dialect of this region." She nodded toward the copy of the parchment. "You should show this to him — he may be able to translate it for you."

Olly and Josh stared at each other in excitement.

"What are we waiting for?" Olly cried, jumping up. "Let's go and talk to Mr. Ram!"

Chapter Five: ☾
Adhita Ram

Olly ran back to the suite to grab Josh's digital camera and to leave a note letting her grandmother know where they had gone. A couple of minutes later, she met up with Josh and Salila outside the front of the palace. Salila had told them that the mahouts led the elephants down to the lake every afternoon — and that Adhita Ram usually went with them. She suggested they go there first, and hopefully save themselves the much longer journey to the orphanage itself.

The road that led to the lake at the base of Elephant Falls wound its way through the hills for several miles, but Salila said she would show them a shortcut, a route that would take them through the hills and forests. That sounded a lot more interesting to Olly and Josh than a long, hot march along a dusty road.

Salila guided them up out of the valley of the Peshwar Palace and down through forests of rosewood and cinnamon trees, where the cool, shaded air was heavy with fragrance and the noise of insects. There were tall chestnut trees, too, and plum trees with branches heavy with fruit. In open country, thick bushes of juniper grew everywhere.

Josh pointed into the sky, to several long, elegant shapes that were moving above the hills with slow wing-beats. "Flamingos!" he cried.

"They are heading toward the sea," Salila explained. "They travel many miles to reach their breeding places."

Josh raced up to a rocky high point to take some pictures as the large, exotic birds with their vivid, pink plumage flew past.

Olly looked at Salila. "Are there any tigers around here?" she asked.

Salila shook her head. "They live farther up in the mountains — away from people," she said. "Higher up there are bears and deer and snow leopards. But where there are people, only wild dogs and monkeys are at home."

Olly sighed. "I'd love to see a snow leopard," she said wistfully.

"I have never seen one," Salila told her. "They are very rare."

The two girls carried on walking. It was a few moments before Olly noticed that Josh had not followed them.

She looked back to the ridge on which he was standing.

"Josh!" she called. "Come on — the flamingos are gone."

Josh didn't reply. He didn't even turn to look at her. Puzzled, Olly marched back toward him. "What are you doing?" she asked.

"Don't come any closer," Josh hissed at her through gritted teeth. "Go and get help."

Then she realized how strangely stiff he was, and noticed that his eyes were fixed on something on the ground just in front of him. She followed his gaze and her heart skipped a beat. A long, sand-yellow snake was rearing up from a nest of stones, its wide hood extended, its forked tongue flickering.

"It's a cobra," Olly breathed. "Josh, don't move!"

"Do I look like I'm moving?" Josh murmured.

"I'll get Salila. She'll know what to do."

Olly ran back to where the Indian girl was waiting. "Josh is face-to-face with a cobra," she gasped.

Without speaking, Salila moved quickly up the hill to where Josh stood frozen with fear. She stepped carefully up to his side and peered closely at the snake. "It is not a cobra," she said after a moment, with a grin. "It is a rat snake. It is harmless."

Josh let out a sigh of relief and backed away from the snake, wiping his sleeve across his forehead.

Olly shook her head. "Way to think it was a cobra," she said, laughing as the snake dropped to the ground and slinked away.

Josh gave her a look. "*You* thought it was a cobra, too," he reminded her.

"Rat snakes look very similar to cobras," Salila told them. "People are easily fooled. But rat snakes have no venom."

Olly looked at her. "*Are* there cobras around here?" she asked.

Salila smiled. "Oh, yes," she said. "It is wise to be careful where you place your feet."

They continued their journey, but after that, Olly found she couldn't take her eyes off the ground. She had a horrible feeling that at any moment something slithery and poisonous would rise up in front of her.

"The best way to deal with a snake is with a mongoose," Josh commented. "Mongooses eat snakes."

"Is that so?" Olly asked. "And do you happen to have a mongoose on you?"

"Not right now," Josh admitted.

"I didn't think so," Olly responded, and returned to her study of the paths ahead.

A loud chattering noise finally broke Olly's obsession with snakes.

She looked up to see a group of monkeys gathered on a rock just ahead of them. She guessed there were about twenty, a whole family troop of adults and babies.

"Those are the monkeys that Jonathan warned us to be careful about," Josh said. "The ones that steal stuff."

Olly looked at the monkeys. "Hey, listen," she called to them. "We've got no food for you guys to steal, all right?"

The monkeys were quite small — the largest of them was probably no taller than knee height — with long, slender tails. They had rough gray-brown fur and small, intelligent faces with big, dark, watchful eyes.

Olly looked at Josh. "Lend me the camera and go and stand over there," she said, pointing at the monkeys.

Josh handed her the camera and walked toward the rock. The monkeys stared at him inquisitively, and a few of the braver ones bounded over to check him out.

Olly held the camera to her eye. "Smile! That's a great pose," she said, giggling. "Josh and the monkeys — I wonder if anyone will be able to tell which is which!"

"Very funny," Josh replied with a hint of a smile.

∿∿∿

It was warm work, trekking through the hills on a hot afternoon, but Olly loved every minute of it. This was far more interesting than sitting in the stuffy conference room listening to the archaeologists disagreeing with one another.

It was mid-afternoon when they crested the last grass-tufted hill and found themselves gazing out at the dramatic spectacle of Elephant Falls.

"There they are!" Olly said, pointing along the lake to where a group of six elephants were drinking and bathing in the shallow water.

Salila shielded her eyes against the sun. "Adhita Ram is with them," she declared.

Eagerly, they climbed down the hill and made their way toward the elephants. The huge beasts seemed to be having a marvelous time in the shallows of the lake. The adults stood knee-deep in the water, filling their trunks and then lifting them high over their heads to send great spouts of water shooting over their backs. The young calves splashed about with water up to their shoulders, their trunks lifted like snorkels.

"They're taking showers." Olly laughed. "And look at that one taking a bath!" One of the elephants was lying on its side in the water while a young mahout scrubbed its mountainous hide with a broom.

"How close can I get to them?" Olly asked Salila.

"They are all tame," Salila told her. "They will not harm you." She called out in her own language to a young boy seated astride the neck of a massive old tusker. The boy kicked his heels and spoke to the elephant, and the creature slowly turned and moved ponderously through the water toward Olly. Its long mobile trunk reached out, its eyes small and strangely gentle in the great, gray head.

Olly stood quite still, captivated and just a little alarmed as the massive bulk of the elephant loomed over her. She held her breath as it examined her with its trunk. Then she reached out cautiously and patted the elephant's thick, tough skin. "I think he likes me!" She laughed, grinning at Josh.

"Most of them are fully grown," Josh said to Salila. "I thought an orphanage would just be for babies."

"The orphanage also looks after old elephants

who can no longer work," Salila explained. "They are brought here from the logging companies and from the mines in the east."

"Good boy!" Olly said, patting the elephant's thick trunk. "I'd love to take you home, but I don't think Gran would approve." She looked at Salila. "So, where's Mr. Ram?" she asked. As much as she was fascinated by the elephants, she had not forgotten their real reason for coming here, and she was eager to find out if Adhita Ram would be able to help them decipher the old parchment.

Salila led them to a hillock where an old man sat watching the elephants with bright eyes. He was very thin and his skin was dark brown, like old leather. His hair and beard were long and gray, and he wore a lungi — a long tunic of faded yellow cotton. Around his wrinkled neck was a necklace of dark brown bodhi beads and on his forehead were two white lines.

Salila introduced Olly and Josh. "My friends have a copy of some very old writings," she explained. "Would you look at it for them, please?"

The old man's bright eyes rested thoughtfully on Olly and Josh. Then a slow smile spread across his wrinkled face. "It will be my pleasure to help your friends," he said, his voice high and breathy.

"Thank you very much," Josh replied, unfolding the sheet of paper and handing it to him.

The old man held it close to his face in both hands. There was silence for a long time. Olly and Josh looked at each other.

"My great-grandfather was a great scholar," the old man said at last. "He would have been able to find the meaning in these words."

Olly looked hopefully at him. "But can you make sense of anything at all?" she asked.

The old man rested the sheet of paper on his bony knees and ran a long, crooked finger down the script. "This section says something like: *When all is lost, turn the key in the lock in the ear*," he murmured. "I believe those are the words, but its meaning is not clear to me. It may be symbolic. The lock may be ignorance. The key may be words of wisdom spoken into the ear to eliminate ignorance."

"I think I know what you mean," Olly said. "But we found an old pottery elephant with a slot behind its ear and there was a key inside it — an actual key. Could that be what it refers to?"

"It is possible," Adhita Ram agreed.

"Can you read anything else?" Josh asked eagerly.

The old man scrutinized the paper again. "Some of these words are familiar to me," he said. "But I have not seen writing like this since I was a small boy, and even then it was on a very ancient document." He shook his head. "I cannot translate anything else for you now. The meanings, the old words, they may come back to me — but it could take many days, and even then I would not be able to translate all of this writing." He held out the paper to Josh. "I am sorry."

"Please keep it," Olly told him, smiling. "Maybe you'll remember some more words later on. We can come back again another day — if you don't mind."

Adhita Ram bowed his head. "You are most welcome to return," he said.

Olly felt hopeful that he might be able to translate more words given time. She stood up, looking over at the elephants. "Do you think it would be OK for us to help give the elephants a bath?"

"Of course, my friend." Adhita Ram laughed. "But be warned — the elephants can be playful."

"So can I," Olly replied with a grin. "Come on, Josh — last one to wash an elephant has to sit by Ethan at dinner!"

Josh gave her a questioning look. Were they having dinner with Ethan? Not wanting to risk it, Josh picked up one of the brooms and ran down to the lake.

Chapter Six: ☾
Trouble at the Temple

It was early the following morning, and Olly was yanked out of a deep sleep by someone roughly shaking her shoulder.

Josh's voice sounded loudly in her ear. "Wake up!"

Olly opened her bleary eyes. "Go away!" she mumbled, trying to pull the covers up over her head. "What time is it?"

"Seven o'clock."

"Leave me alone!" Olly grumbled. "I'm not getting up yet. It's still the middle of the night!"

"OK, suit yourself," Josh replied. "I'll just tell the professor you'll see him later then?"

"What professor?" Olly demanded. "What are you talking about?"

Josh's voice was coming from the other side of the room now. "Your dad!" he called. "He just got here."

All the sleepiness fell away from Olly in an instant. She sat bolt upright in bed. "Why didn't you say so in the first place?" she exclaimed, clambering out from under the sheets.

"We're next door, having breakfast," Josh told her. And with that he was gone.

Olly ran into her bathroom. She splashed some cold water on her face and scrambled into her clothes. A couple of minutes later she came out into the sitting room, eager to see her father.

Professor Christie, Jonathan, Mrs. Beckmann, and Josh were seated at the table, eating breakfast.

Olly's heart lifted at the sight of her father. As always, his gray hair was an untidy thatch and his clothes were rumpled and unkempt. His glasses hung from a cord around his neck, and his corner of the breakfast table was scattered with documents.

He lived in a world of dusty books and ancient artifacts and deep thought, and when he was absorbed by his work — which was most of the time — he paid almost no attention to anything else. If she and her grandmother didn't keep an eye on him, Olly knew he was quite capable of missing meals and of wearing the same clothes for a week.

"Hi, Dad!" Olly said, giving him a quick hug and sitting down next to him. "How was your trip? Did you have time to look at the notes Jonathan made of the meeting yesterday? It just turned into one big argument. I told Ethan that he shouldn't bother starting without you, but no one ever listens to a word I say. You wouldn't think that all those doctors and professors would argue like that. Josh and I gave up in the end. We went to see an old mahout who we thought might be able to translate the parchment. He knew some of the words, but not enough to translate the entire passage. Did they tell you about the elephant with the key inside it?"

"Olly, for heaven's sake," her grandmother said. "Give your father a moment or two to catch his breath, will you? He's only been here ten minutes."

Olly looked from her grandma to her father. "Oh, sorry," she said. "I thought you'd want to know everything that's been going on."

"That's very thoughtful of you, Olivia," Professor Christie said with a smile. "Jonathan sent me his notes of yesterday's meeting and I've been studying the copy of the parchment. It's very interesting."

"Can you read it?" Olly asked. "The only part Mr. Ram could translate for us was about turning a key in someone's ear."

"'When all is lost,'" Josh quoted, "'turn the key in the lock in the ear.'"

Olly looked at her father. "Do you know what that means?"

He shook his head. "I'm afraid I don't," he replied. "But I do recognize some of the words from a document I once read in the museum in Mumbai." He took out a crumpled copy of the parchment, covered with scribbled notes. "This word is *waterfall*, I am almost sure of it," he said, tapping the paper with his forefinger.

Olly frowned. "Does it mean Elephant Falls?" she asked.

"I don't think so," said her father. "I believe it is a reference to something inside the Temple of Ganesha."

"Inside the temple, there's a shrine to Parvati," Jonathan said. "The shrine includes an artificial waterfall."

"But didn't Professor Singh say that the temple had already been searched from top to bottom?" Josh asked.

"I'm sure it has," responded Professor Christie. "But previous archaeologists didn't have the clues that are in the parchment. There are references to the moon, and to a hidden or secret temple." He frowned. "Of course, without being able to put these words in context, it is very difficult to know exactly what they refer to."

"What if it doesn't mean an actual secret temple?" Josh asked. "What if it means a secret *in* a temple?"

"And what if that key we found fits a hidden box in the temple?" Olly added. "The box with the talisman in it!"

"It's an interesting idea," Professor Christie said. "I would like to take a look at the key at some point." His forehead wrinkled. "It's possible that there is an undiscovered temple hidden somewhere in these hills," he said. "There are forested regions and mountain valleys in this area that could be protecting all manner of undiscovered treasures. All the same, I don't know of any documents that specifically mention a lost temple around here."

"So do you think we should concentrate on searching the Temple of Ganesha again?" Jonathan asked.

"I certainly think it makes sense to start our work in there," said the professor. "And this time, I think we should pay particular attention to the shrine to Parvati and its waterfall."

"I'm afraid you won't be able to visit the temple today," said Mrs. Beckmann. She looked at Jonathan. "Don't you remember? The director of your mother's movie has special permission to film there today. They're not going to welcome unexpected visitors; it took them several weeks to obtain permission in the first place, and they have only been allowed eight hours for shooting."

"Then we must be patient," said Professor Christie. "The talisman has been lost for millennia; another twenty-four hours won't make much difference." He looked at Jonathan. "And it will give me some time to talk to Professor Singh and the others. There's a great deal of information we need to discuss." He pushed his chair back. "And I'd like to see Ethan as soon as possible."

"I'll call him," Jonathan said, getting up. "I'm sure he'll want to speak with you, too."

"Can we come?" Olly asked.

"I think not," Mrs. Beckmann broke in before the professor could speak. "I let you skip your lessons yesterday to go to the meeting — and you left halfway through."

"Only because it was so boring," Olly pointed out. "It's not like we were learning anything in there."

Her grandma smiled. "Well, I can assure you that you'll learn something in here," she said, eyeing them both. "Be ready with your books in fifteen minutes, please." She got up and went to her room.

Jonathan called Ethan Cain's suite and Olly and Josh heard him making arrangements for an early morning meeting with Ethan.

A few minutes later, the friends found themselves alone at the table, picking at the last of the breakfast. Olly was thoughtful as she gazed out of the tall windows.

"It will be great if Mr. Ram can decipher some more of that writing," Josh said. "I think we could really be onto something there."

Olly frowned. "What makes you think we aren't already?" she asked.

Josh looked at her. "Because the only part he understood was about a key going into an ear. It's pretty obvious it meant that someone had hidden the key in that pottery elephant's ear. And we already knew that."

Olly shook her head. "I'm not sure that's it," she said. "I've been thinking about it ever since we met Mr. Ram." She looked at Josh. "The key we found came out from *behind* the elephant's ear."

"So?" Josh said. "It had to be put there in the first place, didn't it?"

"Yes, but the point is it was put in *behind* the ear, not *in* it," Olly insisted. "And it was a slot, not a lock." She took a deep breath. "Do you remember what Mr. Ram said? He thought that the passage in the parchment might not mean an actual key, he thought it might just have to do with someone whispering secrets into someone else's ear. We didn't agree with that explanation, because we'd just found a real key. But what if we're both right?"

Josh shook his head. "You've lost me, Olly."

"Maybe that picture of a shrew whispering secrets into an elephant's ear isn't a clue to where the key was *hidden*," she said. "Maybe it's a clue for what you should do with the key once you've found it!"

"You mean it's telling us to use the key in a lock in an elephant's ear — and that will reveal a big secret," Josh breathed. "Like where we could find the talisman!"

"That's right," Olly said. "The pottery elephant that we found the key in doesn't have a lock in its ear — I've double checked. That means we need to find another elephant — one that *does* have a lock in its ear."

"And it might not be an *ordinary* elephant at all," Josh added. "Maybe the lock is in the ear of Ganesha, the elephant-headed god."

"And if we add to that the other clues in the parchment," Olly said. "The waterfall, the secret in the temple — what happens when we put everything together?"

"All the clues seem to point toward the Temple of Ganesha," Josh replied. "That's where the talisman must be hidden. And we can find it by using the key in a lock in an elephant's ear!" He let out a groan of frustration. "Why did we ever let Ethan get his hands on that key?"

"Forget about that for now," Olly said. "What we need is some way of proving whether our theory is correct. If it is, then we can tell Dad about it, and he'll be able to get to the talisman first." She looked anxiously at Josh. "We have to go to the temple and check out any elephant ears in there, either attached to actual elephants, or to Ganesha himself."

"I've seen photos of the temple," Josh said. "It's *full* of carvings and statues of Ganesha."

"But it's still just a process of elimination," Olly pointed out. "We only need to find the one with the keyhole in its ear." She looked at him. "It's a shame we can't go there today, but the place will be full of the cast and crew of the movie."

"So what?" Josh said. "My mom is the costar — if that doesn't get us an on-location pass, then nothing will. And once we're in there, we can search around quietly while everyone else is busy making the movie."

Olly nodded. "There's just one problem," she said. Josh frowned. "What?"

A door opened and Mrs. Beckmann's voice

drifted through from the adjoining room. "If you've finished breakfast, we can start lessons."

"That!" Olly said under her breath.

~~~~~

Josh and Olly knew it would be a waste of time to try and convince Mrs. Beckmann to let them out of lessons. They would just have to submit to classwork for a few hours, and then quietly slip up the hillside to the temple at the first opportunity.

The Temple of Ganesha had been carved long, long ago, in the face of a rocky cliff about a mile north of the Peshwar Palace. Olly and Josh arrived there in the early afternoon to find the area outside the temple blocked by a jumble of trucks, trailers, and jeeps.

"I can't believe how many people it takes to make a movie!" Olly exclaimed, staring at the chaos of vehicles and people.

Josh laughed. He had been on location with his mother before. He knew all about the need for drivers, caterers, carpenters, electricians, camera operators, makeup artists, and props managers — and that was only the start. And there they all were — scurrying around outside the ancient temple like a bunch of frantic ants.

And there was equipment everywhere —

scaffolding and lighting rigs, sound-booms, power generators, and metal tracking for the cameras to run on. Plus, there were the true necessities: massive urns of tea and coffee.

Josh took the lead as the two friends made their way to the temple's square entrance. Above and around the doorway were astonishingly detailed carvings. Figures of men and women, animals, and gods gazed out of the cliff face. They were so skillfully chipped from the gray rock that they seemed almost real — as if caught and frozen in motion centuries ago.

There were people in the open doorway, and a loud voice could be heard from inside. Josh recognized the voice at once: The director, Giovanni Bosconi, was having a fit — or a breakdown — by the sound of it. Josh's mother had shared several stories about how Mr. Bosconi would fly into a tirade if something went wrong in the middle of a scene.

"This isn't working at all," he was shouting now. "The lighting's all wrong. Where's David? I can't work with these lights; they're too bright. I need more shadows. Am I surrounded by amateurs here?"

Olly and Josh slipped inside. The temple was crammed with even more people.

"Give me ten minutes," a gray-haired man was saying to Mr. Bosconi. "I'll fix it."

Josh recognized a young woman standing nearby. She was a production assistant. She turned and smiled at the friends, leaning forward to say in a whisper, "David Starr has two Oscars. He's brilliant, but Giovanni still isn't satisfied. He's driving everyone crazy."

"Where's my mom?" Josh whispered back.

The woman pointed deep into the temple. Natasha Welles and Ben Wilder were being given a quick touch-up by the makeup artists.

"Can we go in, if we keep really quiet?" Josh asked.

"I shouldn't let you," said the woman. "But, since you are the star's son . . ." She smiled. "Just stay out of trouble and don't let Giovanni see you."

Josh and Olly crept along the wall. Even though it was filled with people and gear, the temple was an astonishing sight. Sunlight poured in through high, arched windows, bathing everything in a rich, warm light. The main chamber was a great square room with orange-painted walls. A stone balcony carved with dancing figures stretched across the width of the roof. In the center was the sculpted elephant head of Ganesha, circled with garlands of flowers and beads.

The far end of the chamber was dominated by a six-foot-high full statue of the elephant-headed god. There was a tall golden crown on his head, and his trunk was adorned with a golden shield. He was seated on a stone platform that stood atop a long flight of wide stone steps. Ganesha sat with his four arms raised in blessing, his skin was painted a vivid red, and the expression in his large, black eyes was wise and peaceful. Carved white flowers hung in wreaths around his shoulders.

The friends worked their way to the back of the chamber. Here, a narrow passageway led to the black, wrought-iron gates that marked the entrance of the shrine to Parvati. Josh paused. One of the gates was slightly ajar. He peered inside.

The shrine was quite small and austere compared to the main sanctum. It was just a simple, unadorned chamber, carved from the dark rock. In the far wall, reached by four broad, black, stone steps, was a statue of Parvati, Ganesha's mother. She stood on the edge of a small, rocky precipice, over which a stream of clear water plunged into a wide, oval bowl. Black stone elephants had been carved all around the rim of the bowl; each had a lighted candle flickering in a holder on its back. More elephants stood underneath the bowl, as though bearing its weight on their shoulders.

A narrow sunbeam splashed in a pool of light on the stone floor. Josh couldn't see where the sunbeam was coming from, but he realized there must be some kind of window or vent high up near the roof. The pool of sunlight threw the rest of the shrine into deep shade, but the ring of stumpy yellow candles gave off a soft glow that scattered the shadows and flickered over the dark rock.

The shrine was very peaceful and calming. But then, to Josh's surprise, he saw a third source of light in the shrine. It was a flashlight! A man was running the beam of the flashlight over the elephants around the rim of the bowl. It was as if he was searching for something.

Josh caught his breath and shrank back in the shadows. It was Ethan Cain.

Josh heard Olly's voice softly in his ear. "What's he doing here?" she asked.

Josh shook his head and gestured for Olly to back up so they could speak without fear of Ethan overhearing them. So far, he was unaware of their presence — absorbed as he was in carefully examining each of the black, stone elephants in turn.

"I thought he was supposed to be chairing another one of those meetings this afternoon," Olly said quietly. "What's he doing up here?" She peeped through the gateway. "He's looking at the elephants," she added. "Why would he be doing that?"

"Someone must have told him what Mr. Ram said," Josh replied in a low voice. "He must have come to the same conclusion as we did about the key. He's looking for the elephant's ear with the keyhole in it. But why is he in here on his own?"

"Because he'd rather find the talisman all on his own, if he can," Olly muttered darkly. "I bet the others don't even know he's here." She frowned. "We can't search the shrine now — not while he's poking about in there." Her eyes glinted. "So, what do we do instead?"

Josh beckoned for her to follow him back the way they had come. "The ear with the keyhole in it might not be in the shrine to Parvati at all," he pointed out to Olly. "It could be anywhere in the temple." He looked up. "It could even be up there," he said, pointing at the sculpted head of Ganesha carved in the center of the long balcony.

Olly looked up at the balcony. "So let's go and check it out."

Narrow stone stairs wound up to the high balcony. Olly led the way this time. From up there, deep in shadows under the roof, Josh could see the movie crew getting ready for a reshoot. He peered down. His mother and Ben Wilder were being given instructions by Giovanni Bosconi. Camera operators were standing by.

Olly crept toward the middle of the balcony with Josh close behind. She leaned over the stone banister. Unfortunately, the elephant head was located at the base of the balcony, so they had to lean over the banister to even see the top of its ears.

"Can you see anything?" Josh hissed.

"It's too dark," Olly replied. She drew back. "I think I can squeeze between these," she said, edging a shoulder between the stone columns that supported the banister rail. "Then I'll be able to get closer. But you'll have to keep hold of me in case I slip."

"Are you sure about this?" Josh whispered uneasily. "That would be a nasty fall."

Olly looked at him. "Then don't drop me," she instructed.

She eased her head and shoulders between the stone pillars and squirmed around so she was on her stomach. Josh hooked his fingers into her belt, taking her weight as she edged forward to inspect the carved head.

"OK, everyone," Giovanni Bosconi called. "Scene fifty-seven, take fifteen. All quiet on set, please. I want plenty of energy, Natasha and Ben! OK — *action!*"

The assistant director snapped the clapper board.

Josh leaned forward to see what was going on down below. Ben and his mother were crouching behind the stone platform of Ganesha's statue. A strong flashlight beam was being shone around the temple from behind the cameras. The two actors ducked down as the light passed near them. Obviously, someone was searching for them in the scene.

Olly edged out a little farther. Josh tightened his grip on her belt. The beam of the flashlight slid over the walls of the temple and Josh watched the cameras follow it.

Suddenly, the flashlight beam climbed the wall and raked the balcony. Josh's heart jumped into his mouth — the beam of light was coming right toward them.

"Cut!" the director bellowed furiously.

Olly was caught on camera, right in the glare of the flashlight beam.

"What is going on up there?" Giovanni Bosconi yelled. "Who are those kids?"

"Oh, hi!" Olly called down. "Sorry — did I mess up your shot?"

~~~~

Olly and Josh stood just outside the ring of trucks and jeeps. Olly was staring at the temple, her face clouded and her hands on her hips. "Anyone would think I'd ruined his precious shot on purpose," she moaned. "I told him it was a total accident — but would he listen?"

"I think we're lucky he didn't strangle us both with his bare hands," Josh remarked.

"He shouted at me!" Olly exclaimed. "I don't like being shouted at. I should go back in there and give him a piece of my mind."

Josh grabbed her arm. "Don't do that," he said. "We're going to be in enough trouble with my mom as it is, without you making it worse."

"Ethan Cain is still in there hunting for the key-hole," Olly snapped. "And he has the silver key, so he can open the lock the moment he finds it and grab the talisman for himself!" She stalked off angrily. "How could things possibly be any worse?"

Chapter Seven: ☾
Making Movies,
Keeping Secrets

The sun was setting, huge and orange on a golden horizon. A warm breeze wafted in from the palace gardens, scented with roses, hyacinths, and honeysuckle. Stars were just beginning to appear in the darkening sky and traditional Indian music was playing softly. A woman's voice rang out above the fluid, plaintive accompaniment of plucked sitar strings and the hypnotic rhythm of tabla drums.

Torches had been lit out on the dining-room balcony. Their flickering flames made the shadows dance. Around the table sat the entire Christie party, along with their special guest for the evening, Natasha Welles. Ethan had also joined them for the meal, but his dutiful assistant, Mr. White, had arrived at the table after only a few minutes, to say that Ethan was needed urgently on the phone. Some big problem had arisen at the headquarters of Ethan's California-based computer company.

"This could take a while," Ethan had said, apologizing. "I may not be able to get back any time soon. Enjoy your meal."

Olly wasn't sorry to see him go, but she was delighted to know that he had obviously found nothing in the temple that afternoon — his dour mood was proof of that.

There was more good news for the friends, too. Natasha wasn't angry with them for the trouble they had caused on the set. Quite the opposite, in fact. To Olly's surprise, Natasha seemed to find the whole incident highly entertaining.

"And then Olly said, 'Sorry, did I mess up your shot?'" quoted Natasha, shaking with laughter as she related the story. "Giovanni went absolutely crazy."

"It was a complete accident!" Olly exclaimed indignantly. "But he just yelled and threw us out before I could explain."

"Leave it to Olly," Jonathan sighed, grinning. "If there's an ounce of opportunity for trouble, she will find it."

"I hope you apologized properly to Mr. Bosconi," Mrs. Beckmann said, frowning.

Olly looked sheepishly at her grandmother, who obviously didn't find this nearly as amusing as Natasha or Jonathan did.

"We tried to," Josh said. "But he wasn't really listening."

"He didn't give us a chance," Olly agreed. "He was jumping around and waving his arms in the air and yelling so much that we couldn't get a word in edgewise." She looked at Natasha. "Did he *ever* calm down? We really didn't mean to wreck his shot."

Natasha smiled. "Don't worry about it," she replied. "That man is never calm. He's been driving me crazy. We were shooting a really simple scene a few weeks ago, in which my character realizes that her friend is actually working for the bad guys and was wearing a wire — you know, a bug that recorded everything I said and transmitted it to the bad guys who were listening in a van nearby. We only had a few lines of dialogue between us, and then I had to walk out of the room. But Giovanni kept changing his mind about how he wanted to shoot the scene. We ended up spending two whole days on it!" She shook her head. "And the version he used in the end was the very first one we did." She looked at Olly and Josh. "*That's* why I didn't mind you driving *him* crazy for once. He deserved it!"

"All the same, Natasha," Mrs. Beckmann put in. "I really don't think we want a repeat performance." She gave Olly and Josh a fierce look. "Do we?"

"I don't think they'll get the chance." Natasha laughed. "Despite Olly's surprise guest appearance, Giovanni got all the footage he needed. In fact, we're almost done. There are just a few scenes to be shot down in Tauri, then principal photography will be finished." She smiled around the table. "I've convinced the producers to hold the wrap party — to celebrate the end of filming — right here in the Peshwar Palace. And you're all invited. It's in three days. There will be reporters, TV cameras, everything! It should be a glamorous affair."

Professor Christie frowned at her. "I hope it won't turn into a media circus, Natasha," he said. "I don't want our work disrupted by reporters."

"I promise they won't get in your way, Kenneth," Natasha said, flashing him a dazzling smile. "But you know what they say — there's no such thing as bad publicity."

The professor gave her a horrified look.

"Don't worry about it, Dad," Olly reassured him. "The party's not for another three days — we might have found the talisman by then."

"I think you're jumping the gun a little, there," Jonathan said. "I suspect the film crew will be long gone before we get anywhere close to unraveling the text on that old parchment."

"I'm afraid Jonathan is probably right," Professor Christie agreed.

"But you already know some of the words," Josh said eagerly. "It won't take you long to put it all together, will it?"

"That's easier said than done," said the professor, shaking his head. "Without knowing the grammar of the language, the individual words can only offer glimpses into the meaning. Thanks to Olly and Josh, Adhita Ram has shed some light on one section — if he has translated it correctly — but that isn't enough to help us with the rest. We're still a long way from any real understanding of the text." He sighed. "And my colleagues have differing opinions about how we should proceed. I'm hoping that I will be able to convince them to explore the Temple of Ganesha tomorrow."

"I'm sure Ethan will be on your side," Natasha said. "He has a tremendous amount of respect for you, Kenneth."

Olly rolled her eyes at Josh, who gave her a sympathetic look. They both knew exactly how much respect Ethan Cain had for the professor! Just enough to use him to hunt down the talisman and then snatch it out from under his nose at the last moment.

"I wanted to ask you something. My costar, Ben Wilder, is a talented amateur archaeologist," Natasha was saying. She looked at Professor Christie. "He wondered if it would be possible for him to film you while he's here — to make a record of the hunt for the talisman."

"I don't see why not," Professor Christie said. "If he is careful not to get in the way of our work."

"You won't even know he's there," Natasha promised. "And just think — it means you'll have a day-by-day record of your search."

"Natasha's right, Dad," Olly said eagerly. "Wouldn't it be great to have someone right there with a camera when we find the Elephant of Parvati?"

The professor smiled at Olly, then turned to Natasha. "Tell Ben that he's welcome to join us, as far as I'm concerned," he said. "But Ethan will have to give his blessing, of course. He's in charge of this conference."

Natasha smiled. "I've already asked Ethan," she replied. "He said it was fine with him — but only if you approved. Ben will be really pleased. He's not needed on set tomorrow, so if you really are going to explore the temple, I'm sure he'd love to be there."

"Don't forget to take the silver key with you," Olly reminded her father. "Then, when you find the ear with the keyhole in it, you'll be able to open it right away."

"Professor Singh has explored the temple on several occasions," her father said. "She is adamant that there isn't any kind of hidden keyhole in there."

"Not even in the shrine?" Olly asked. "Josh and I have this theory that the keyhole is probably in Parvati's shrine."

"And why's that?" Jonathan asked.

"Well, it's obvious, isn't it?" Olly responded. "Dad said that the parchment mentioned a waterfall, and the only waterfall around here — apart from Elephant Falls — is in the shrine to Parvati. So the talisman is probably there."

"I see," Mrs. Beckmann said, looking grave. "I assume *that* was the real reason you went up there this afternoon. And you told me you just wanted to watch the movie being shot."

Olly smiled weakly at her. "Well, we did want to see the movie being made," she insisted. "We just thought we could look for the keyhole at the same time. You know, multitasking."

Jonathan laughed. "But if you thought the keyhole was in the shrine," he said, "why were you hanging from the balcony in the main chamber?"

"Because Ethan was in the shrine," Olly explained.

"And we didn't want to disturb him," Josh added quickly. "Do you know why Ethan was there?"

Jonathan shook his head. "He handed the meeting over to the professor after lunch," he said. "But I thought he had been called away because of some problem in California. I didn't know he had gone up to the temple."

"But it was you who told him what Adhita Ram had said, wasn't it?" Olly asked.

"Not me," he said. "I never had a chance to mention it."

Olly looked at her father. "Did you discuss it with him, Dad?" she asked.

Professor Christie shook his head.

"Why do you ask?" Jonathan inquired.

"Oh, no reason," Olly replied, glancing at Josh. "It's not important."

But it was very strange. She and Josh had only decided to investigate the shrine after making the link between the shrew whispering to the elephant and Adhita Ram's translation about putting a key into a lock in an ear. If no one had told Ethan Cain of the old mahout's words, then why had he been in the shrine that afternoon? And why had he been so interested in the elephants there?

It was a real puzzle.

Chapter Eight: ☾
The Hidden Temple

The meal was over. Josh and Olly sat alone on the steps down to the gardens, while the others chatted over drinks at the table.

A starry night had fallen over the valley, and the long gardens were a sea of shadows, surrounding ponds that reflected sparkling stars. The hills looked like the black backs of sleeping animals and the walls of the palace glowed with light.

Olly sipped her badan, a sweet drink made from almonds and saffron-flavored milk. Josh had chosen a masala soda, flavored with lime and spices.

"So," Olly said, her voice low so she would not be overheard at the nearby table. "How come Ethan Cain was up there checking out the elephants, if no one told him what Adhita Ram said to us?"

"Maybe Ethan heard about Mr. Ram," Josh suggested. "Maybe Ethan went and talked to him."

"I suppose that could be it," Olly agreed. "Listen, we told Mr. Ram we'd go and visit him again soon. Perhaps we should do that tomorrow — that way we can ask him whether Ethan sneaked over to worm information out of him."

"Shouldn't we go back to the temple first to try and find the keyhole?" Josh asked. "I know no one else believes it's there, but I don't think they've looked hard enough."

Olly nodded. "I agree," she said. "It's got to be there. OK, first of all, we go up to the temple with Dad and the others. If we can't find the keyhole, then we go and see Mr. Ram. He might have deciphered some more of the writing. But even if he hasn't, at least we can warn him not to talk to Ethan again."

Josh looked thoughtfully at her.

"What?" she asked.

"Oh, nothing," he said. "I was just wondering whether your grandmother would let us out of lessons in the morning, that's all."

Olly stared at him. "Of course she will," she said. "Exploring the temple is educational, isn't it? How could she refuse?"

〰〰〰

It was the following morning. Breakfast had been cleared away and Professor Christie and Jonathan had gone to make preparations for their trip to the temple. Olly went into her bedroom and emerged wearing her hill-trekking clothes and a pair of stout walking boots.

Mrs. Beckmann was having a final cup of tea and reading the newspaper. Josh was leaning on the balcony, enjoying the view.

Olly stood in the open balcony doorway. "Come on, Josh, get your gear. We're not going to wait for you."

Mrs. Beckmann peered at Olly over the top of the newspaper. "And where exactly do you think you're going, Olivia?" she asked.

Olly turned cheerfully to look at her grandmother. "Josh and I are going to help explore the temple," she said. She gave her grandmother a hopeful smile. "It'll be really educational. A once-in-a-lifetime experience. We'll tell you all about it when we get back. We could even write up a report."

Mrs. Beckmann finished her tea and quietly folded the paper. "I expect you to be ready for your lessons in fifteen minutes," she said.

Olly laughed. "Very funny, Gran."

Mrs. Beckmann raised an eyebrow.

Olly looked to Josh for support, but he had an I-told-you-so expression on his face.

Olly took a deep breath. "OK," she said. "Can we make a deal, Gran? Double lessons tomorrow if you let us off today? We really have to go to the temple with Dad."

Mrs. Beckmann stood up. "I'm sure he will still be there when your lessons are finished," she replied. "And so will the temple. Now, take those boots off, Olly, and get your books. Lessons start in ten minutes."

And that was her final word on the subject.

~~~~

Mrs. Beckmann had been right about one thing, as Olly could clearly see when she and Josh arrived at the Temple of Ganesha. There were three jeeps parked outside the entrance — the archaeologists were all still there.

Now that the trucks and other movie gear were gone, Olly could really appreciate the workmanship that had gone into carving the temple facade. She gazed up at the figures of humans, animals, and gods. The detail in the carvings was dazzling.

The two friends walked in under the square entrance. Jonathan was standing just inside, studying wall carvings and making notes. From deeper inside the temple, Olly could hear the sound of voices.

"I hope you haven't found the talisman without us," Olly said.

Jonathan gave a half smile. "Not yet, I'm afraid," he replied.

"Can we go in?" Josh asked.

"Of course," Jonathan told him. "This is a fascinating place — we've already found out a lot about it." He pointed to a carved inscription. "The temple was put together in three distinct stages over almost two thousand years, but there's something even more interesting. The earliest inscriptions say that the first stage of the building involved carving the temple out of caves that had already been used for worship for many centuries."

Jonathan led them into the main body of the temple. Over by the tunnel that led to the shrine to Parvati stood a group of archaeologists. An intense, but outwardly polite, debate was going on.

Olly noticed that someone was missing. "Where's Ethan?" she asked.

"He had to stay behind at the hotel," Jonathan told her, shaking his head. "More business problems in California, I think. I don't know how he manages to find time to organize this conference with all the other responsibilities he has."

"He's just a total superman, I guess," Olly said drily.

Jonathan gave her a sharp look, but she just

smiled innocently and walked up the steps that led to the huge statue of Ganesha.

She gazed around the temple. It seemed larger and more imposing now that the film crew was gone. The place glowed in the light that poured in through the high windows. The elephant-headed deity sat in the middle of the chamber on his stone platform, a strange-looking creature, Olly thought, but also rather magnificent and strangely calming.

"Did you find anything yet?" Josh asked his brother as Olly rose on tiptoe to peer into Ganesha's golden ear.

"Not so far," Jonathan confirmed. He nodded toward the professors. "They're still debating whether there's any point in being here at all. Half of them think it's a waste of time."

Olly moved around to the other side of the statue and looked into Ganesha's other ear. There was no sign of anything resembling a keyhole. "Rats," she breathed. "This is so annoying!"

"Still looking for the keyhole, Olly?" Jonathan asked. "It's not here, I promise you."

Olly frowned. "All the same, is it OK for us to look for it?" she said. "Just in case it was missed."

Jonathan smiled. "Be my guest, Olly. I hope you're successful."

The archaeologists were blocking the way to the shrine, so Olly and Josh separated and spent the next half hour exploring the main sanctum. They carefully examined the ears of every elephant, and of every statue and painting of Ganesha. They met together at the far side of the chamber. Neither of them had found anything remotely resembling a keyhole.

The professors had moved outside to continue their discussions, so the friends were now able to make their way along the dark passage that led to the shrine. Josh pushed open the black iron gates and they went inside.

A circle of bright sunlight marked one wall. Olly looked up at the vaulted roof. A high, narrow hole had been carved in the rock, and it was through this opening that the sunlight streamed into the shrine.

Olly felt that the shrine had quite a different atmosphere than the rest of the temple. In spite of the constant splashing of the water into the stone bowl, there was a deep sense of silence. The candles in their sconces on the backs of the elephants gave off a soft, steady yellow glow. A thin trail of smoke rose from an incense holder by the door, scenting the air with sandalwood. The subdued mood of the small chamber made Olly feel like she should whisper.

She went closer to the statue of Parvati herself. The goddess was carved from smooth, shiny black stone. She wore a headdress, and one hand was raised in welcome. There was a peaceful smile on her face, and her bright eyes, reflecting the candle-light, seemed to shine with joyful life.

The fall of clear water poured from a crack in the wall behind the statue of Parvati, and splashed softly into the broad stone basin. Olly couldn't see where the water went after that, but she assumed it flowed away through some hidden pipe. The constant rippling of the water threw reflected light over the dark stone walls, giving the impression that the whole room was deep underwater.

Olly walked slowly around the bowl, examining each elephant in turn. Then she knelt and looked into the ears of the elephants that supported the bowl.

She turned to Josh, who was gazing up into Parvati's lovely face. "There's nothing here," she murmured.

Josh sighed. "Maybe our key really doesn't have anything to do with the talismans," he said.

Olly shook her head. "No," she argued. "I'm not going to accept that — not yet, anyway."

"But we've searched the entire temple," Josh pointed out. "What do we do now?"

"We do what we agreed," Olly told him. "We go and see Mr. Ram again." She gave him a hopeful smile. "You never know — he might have remembered something else."

~~~~~

It wasn't a long trek across the hills to the lake at the foot of Elephant Falls. The elephants from the orphanage were there, wading in the shallows with their mahouts, and cooling themselves off with great spouts of water. Sitting watching them on the same grassy hill as last time was the unmistakeable figure of Adhita Ram.

"Ah, my young friends," he said as Josh and Olly approached. "I am glad you have come — I have some news for you."

Olly's heart jumped. She scrambled up the hill and sat in front of the elderly man. "What is it?" she asked eagerly.

Josh sat beside her, looking hopeful.

The old man drew the crumpled copy of the parchment from his clothing. He pointed to a section of the strange writing at the top of the page. "I think this is an old saying," he told them. "I remember it from a long time ago. It is not used much these days. It says . . ."— his finger moved along the writing as he spoke — "*To see beyond the moonlit veil, the seeker must look without looking.*" He pointed to another section. "And this says: *The seeker must crack the nutshell in order to discover the kernel within.*"

Olly frowned. "I'm sorry," she said. "What do those sayings mean?"

Adhita Ram smiled gently at her. "Only the seeker can answer that question," he replied.

"The seeker of the Elephant of Parvati, you mean?" Josh asked.

"Possibly. I do not know," the old man said. "Only the seeker knows."

Olly looked closely at him. "We're looking for the Elephant of Parvati," she said slowly. "So that makes us the seekers, right?"

Adhita Ram shook his head. "I do not know," he repeated. "Only the seeker knows."

Olly closed her eyes. This was making her head spin.

"Have you managed to figure out what anything else means?" Josh asked.

The old mahout shook his head. "The words are lost to me," he said, making a curious fluttering gesture with his hand, like a bird flying away. "It has been too many years."

"Has anyone else spoken to you about the parchment?" Josh asked.

"No, only you, my friends," Adhita Ram replied.

Olly frowned. "Well, is there anyone else around here who might be able to translate any of it?" she asked.

The old man's face cracked in a wide smile and his long, thin hand came up to touch his chest. "Only Adhita Ram knows," he said proudly. "Only Adhita Ram remembers. No one else remembers. I am the oldest. Only I remember the old words and the old writings." The smile became slightly crooked. "Although Adhita Ram does not remember it all, and for that he is truly sorry."

Olly and Josh exchanged a puzzled look. If Ethan Cain had not spoken to the mahout, then how come they had found him snooping around the elephants in the shrine?

"Don't apologize. You've been really helpful," Olly told the old man. "Honestly, you have."

"I come here to Parvati Falls with the elephants every afternoon," the mahout responded. "Maybe you can come and speak with me again? Maybe I will remember more."

"We'll come again when we can," Olly said. "But please don't worry if you can't remember anything else. We appreciate all your help." She stood up to leave, but she noticed that Josh was still staring at the old man.

"This is *Elephant* Falls, isn't it?" Josh asked. "You just called it *Parvati* Falls."

"It has been called Elephant Falls for many years, because the elephants are brought here to drink and to bathe," Adhita Ram told him. "But in the old days this waterfall was sacred to Parvati. The pilgrims would come here to honor Parvati and to fill the lake with lotus blossoms. It is long forgotten by my people now, but my great-grandfather was a scholar; he read the ancient texts. He told me that there was an old tale of a temple by the waterfall — a temple to Parvati."

Olly's eyes widened. "A temple?" she breathed, gazing around. "Where?"

"The temple was hidden," Adhita Ram replied. "And besides, this was many centuries ago."

"Hidden where?" Josh asked eagerly.

The old man smiled mysteriously and shook his head. "I do not know the answer to that question, my friend," he said. "Maybe only the seeker knows the answer."

Chapter Nine: ☾
An Important Discovery

"So there really is a secret temple," Olly breathed, staring at Josh over the table in the main room of their suite back at the Peshwar Palace. They were alone in the suite, and all was quiet, save for the singing of birds in the gardens and the occasional cry of a peacock.

"You mean there *was*, centuries ago," Josh replied. "There's nothing there now."

Olly frowned. "Even if the temple was torn down — surely there must be some clue to show where it was," she said. "A few stones or some of the foundation. Come on, Josh, you've been on plenty of archaeological expeditions by now. There's always *something* left."

Josh looked at her. "You're assuming that it was made of stone," he said. "Not all temples were. It might have been wooden. There could have been a fire."

Olly shook her head. "If there had been a temple there that was either knocked down or destroyed in a fire, why would Adhita Ram's great-grandfather have referred to it as a *hidden* temple?"

"Hmm, good point," Josh agreed. "It would be more likely to have been called the *lost* temple or something like that. But there are forests and ravines all over this area. We could search for years and never find it — especially if it was hidden in the first place."

"Jonathan told us that the Temple of Ganesha started off as a small cave in the cliffs," Olly said. "But then more people came along and made it bigger and bigger. What if this hidden temple was always just a cave in the cliffs somewhere near the waterfall?"

"And what if there was a landslip or an avalanche?" Josh added excitedly. "And the entrance was blocked. Then, as time went by, people remembered that there used to be a temple there — but they forgot exactly where it was. Olly, you're right. That could be it!"

"And the waterfall mentioned in the parchment might not be the waterfall in the shrine in the Temple of Ganesha. It could be the real waterfall — Elephant Falls," Olly said. "That would explain why we couldn't find the keyhole in the other temple. It's not in the Temple of Ganesha at all — it's in the hidden temple by Elephant Falls.

And *that's* where we'll find the Elephant of Parvati!" A grin spread across her face. "Josh, we are amazing! This hotel is stuffed full of expert archaeologists, but it's the two of us who worked this out!" She laughed. "Ethan will go crazy!"

Josh laughed. "We don't know if we're right yet," he pointed out. "All we've got so far is a good theory. I don't think we should go yelling it from the rooftops just yet. If we tell Jonathan and the professor about this, they'll just go and tell Ethan right away. And then he'll hire a load of digging gear and start searching."

"And when he finds the temple, he'll get all the glory," Olly agreed gloomily. "You're right — we'd just be handing the talisman to him on a plate." She looked at Josh. "But what else can we do? It would take us forever to search the hills near the waterfall. And if the cave is blocked off, we'd never find it anyway without a bulldozer or something."

Josh rested his chin in his hands and stared thoughtfully out the window.

Olly leaned back in her chair, her arms folded over her chest. "It's a pity the people who made that parchment didn't include a map!" she grumbled.

Josh stared at her. "There's a map room downstairs,"

he said. "Some of Oliver Gordon-Howes's maps are down there. And there are some much older maps, too — maps of this area that go back hundreds of years."

Olly looked at him dubiously. "You think there might be a map with an arrow and a little sign saying 'Hidden Temple This Way'?" she said. "I think someone would have noticed it before now, if there was."

"They would if it was like that," Josh agreed. "But remember what Adhita Ram said? It's been centuries since pilgrims came to the temple. But there would have been some kind of road or path that they used. Even if the old maps don't mention the temple, they might still show the old road."

"So, we'd be looking for a roadway that just seems to stop dead at the cliff face somewhere near the waterfall," Olly said thoughtfully. "And if we find it, then we'll know exactly where the temple is. Josh, sometimes you're almost clever!"

"And once we can pinpoint the place," Josh said, "we can tell Jonathan and the professor all about it. Even if Ethan does supply the men and machines to dig the temple out again — everybody will know it was the two of us who found out where it was. And Ethan won't be able to claim it for his own."

"I love it!" Olly crowed. "Let's go and look at the maps right now. Ethan has been ahead of us all the way so far, but this time, we're in the lead."

〰〰〰

The Map Room was on the ground floor of the palace, at the end of a long hallway with walls painted ivory and decorated with peacock feathers and cascades of purple and white flowers.

Josh frowned and caught hold of Olly's wrist as they approached the tall doors of the Map Room.

"What?" she asked, looking at him curiously.

Josh pointed ahead — one of the room's heavy doors was slightly ajar.

Olly walked forward more quietly now. She had a bad feeling about this, although she could not have said exactly why. The room wasn't kept locked — anyone in the hotel could get access to the maps — and the palace was full of archaeologists, any one of whom might decide that a visit to the Map Room would be worthwhile. Still, Olly couldn't escape the feeling that there was something wrong.

A moment later she heard a voice from beyond the doors. She stopped in her tracks and looked at Josh. "That's Ethan's voice," she whispered.

"It can't be," Josh replied.

Olly's eyes narrowed warily as she crept up to the doors. She peered in through the narrow gap.

The Map Room was long, with a high ceiling, and as ornately decorated as were all the rooms in the palace. Tall, arched windows let in a flood of light. Framed maps hung on the walls behind glass. Others were stored safely in heavy cabinets which lined the walls.

Two figures were bending over the open drawer of a cabinet near the center of the far wall, apparently absorbed in studying its contents. Olly recognized the figures immediately: It was Ethan Cain and his assistant, Paul White.

Olly drew back and beckoned for Josh to look, too. Together, the friends watched the two men pore over the maps.

"Do you see anything?" Ethan asked his assistant.

"Nothing," Paul replied.

"Neither do I." Ethan closed the map drawer and opened the one below.

Olly and Josh moved away from the doors.

"What are they doing here?" Josh whispered.

"That's what I'd like to know," Olly hissed. She beckoned for Josh to follow her back along the hallway and out through the dining room. They sat on the steps overlooking the garden.

"There's something weird going on here," Olly said. "This is the third time Ethan has managed to spoil our plans — and I'm getting sick of it!"

Josh nodded. "It's almost as if he knows what we're about to do and gets there first," he said. "We'd only just found the silver key when he turned up out of nowhere. Then he was in the shrine to Parvati ahead of us. And now he's in the Map Room just a few minutes after we decided to go there."

"I can't really see Ethan snooping through keyholes," Olly said. "But how else could he know?"

"It must be a coincidence," Josh said. "A really annoying coincidence."

"*Three* annoying coincidences," Olly reminded him. And then a thought struck her. She looked at Josh. "Remember that story your mom told us the other night? It was about a scene that Giovanni Bosconi made her do over and over again."

Josh frowned. "The scene where she realized that her so-called friend was wearing a microphone," he said. "Yeah, so?"

"What if Ethan has hidden a microphone somewhere in our hotel room?" Olly suggested.

Josh snorted with laughter. "Oh, please!" he said. "What is this, a James Bond movie? You seriously think Ethan bugged our suite?"

"Why not?" Olly demanded. "He's perfectly capable of pulling a dirty trick like that. And it would explain why he's always one step ahead of us. And if you think about it, in each case, we've talked things through in the sitting room up there. We were in that room when we found the silver key. We were in there with Dad and Jonathan when we were talking about Adhita Ram, and we were just there when we said there might be something useful in the Map Room."

Josh gazed at her. "We should go and check," he said firmly.

~~~~~

Olly paused outside the door to their suite. "We have to do this really quietly," she said. "If you find anything, just wave your hand, OK?"

Josh nodded. He didn't really believe that they would find a bug. It seemed too far-fetched an idea, even for Ethan Cain.

Olly opened the door and they walked silently inside. She began to search behind the large wooden cabinet that stood by the door. Josh carefully lifted some pictures down off the walls and checked the backs. He found nothing suspicious.

Josh watched as Olly squeezed herself between two display cabinets and stretched her arm down the back. Then he walked over to the heavy velvet curtains that hung beside the balcony doors. He moved them aside and examined the door frame. Again, he found nothing.

Olly was now stretched full-length over one of the cabinets, reaching down the back, her legs waving in the air. Josh had to stifle a burst of laughter. This was silly — they weren't going to find anything.

He went to the table and ran his hand around under the top. Nothing. *Of course not*, he thought to himself. *There isn't anything here.* And then his fingers touched on something smooth, protruding slightly from the underside of the table.

Josh crouched under the table and peered upward. A small gray object was attached underneath the tabletop, near the center. It wasn't much bigger than a bottle top, it seemed to be made of metal, and it was stuck to the table by some kind of adhesive patch.

Josh realized that he was staring up at an electronic listening device. Olly was right: Ethan Cain really had bugged their room!

Chapter Ten: 🌙
Wild Goose Chase

Olly and Josh crouched together under the table, staring up at the small gray metal disk.

What do we do with it? Olly mouthed silently to Josh. She acted out smashing it, but Josh shook his head. Olly gave him an inquiring look, and he crawled out from under the table, beckoning to her.

She followed him out into the hallway and Josh closed the door firmly behind them. He stared up and down the corridor before speaking in a low, urgent voice.

"If we smash it, he'll know we've found it," he said.

"I don't care," Olly snarled. "I want him to know we've found him out — the big, slimy rat! He's been listening to everything we've said in there right from the start. No wonder he was always one jump ahead of us. He was planning on using us to do all the hard work for him — and then he was just going to stroll off with the Elephant of Parvati after we'd figured out where it was."

Josh nodded. "I'm sure that's exactly what he planned on doing," he said. "But you know what he's like, he'd never admit the bug had anything to do with him." A sly grin spread over his face. "But if we leave it where it is, he won't know we've found it."

Olly looked blankly at him. "So?"

"So, we can have some fun with him," Josh explained. "We can invent some stuff and send him off on a wild goose chase."

Olly's eyes widened in delight. "We can say we know where the talisman is," she breathed, grinning. "Josh, that's a great idea. Let's do it now."

"No, let's wait," Josh argued. "We have to be convincing. Let's do it tomorrow after our schoolwork. We can pretend we've been to see Adhita Ram again, and that he's translated some more of the parchment. In the meantime, we can take a look at a local map, and see if we can find a really good place to send him."

~~~~~

Later in the afternoon, Olly and Josh went down to the Map Room again. This time the doors were closed and the room was empty. They spent half an hour or more pulling out the long shallow drawers and examining the maps. The more recent maps were highly detailed and very accurate — and they showed nothing to indicate either a hidden temple or a pilgrim track anywhere near Elephant Falls. The most ancient maps were several hundred years old, but although they were beautifully drawn — with small colorful pictures and explanations in the old Devanagari script — none seemed to indicate the existence of a temple or an old road near the waterfall.

"There's one good thing about this," Josh pointed out as they left the room. "If we didn't find anything useful, then neither did Ethan."

Olly nodded. "I wonder if Dad and the others are back from the temple yet?" she said. "I'd like to know if they found anything up there." She smiled. "And I'd *really* like to get all those professors together and tell them what we've figured out!"

Josh looked anxious. "We can't do that," he said. "They'll just tell Ethan."

"I know," Olly replied. "Don't worry, I won't breathe a word. I want to see Ethan's face when he finds out that we've outsmarted him again."

~~~~~

The Christie team met up for dinner out on the moonlit balcony of their suite that evening. As Olly and Josh had suspected, the investigations up at the temple had not been particularly successful.

While they ate, Olly and Josh looked at some printouts of digital photographs that Jonathan had taken of the temple and the shrine.

Professor Christie spent most of the meal going through his notebook, reading and rereading the notes he had been making ever since he arrived in India.

"Kenneth, you must eat something," Olly's grandmother told him eventually.

He gazed distractedly at her. "Hmmm?"

"Eat some food," she said. "You'll waste away."

Olly smiled fondly at her father — when he was on the track of an elusive piece of information, it was as if he were on another planet.

Nibbling at a popadum, Olly flicked through the printed digital photographs. She spread out a few pictures of the shrine.

"It's weird that they bothered to cut that little window through all that rock," she murmured, looking at the white pool of sunlight that glowed on the wall. "I mean, it's not like it lets much useful light in," she continued. "You still need candles in there to actually see anything."

She looked up. Her father was staring at her. "What?" she said. "What did I say?"

He didn't reply. Now everyone at the table was looking at him.

"Professor?" Jonathan asked. "What is it?"

Without answering, Professor Christie turned to a clean sheet in his notebook and began to draw. As he worked, Olly saw a look of understanding and delight come over his face.

"Dad!" she demanded. "What's going on?"

He looked up at her, smiling widely. "Well done, Olly!" he declared. "It's been staring me in the face all along, but I didn't make the connection till you mentioned it." He turned the notebook around to show them the sketch he had made. It was rough, but Olly could see that it was Parvati's shrine. It showed the little window in the roof, from which her father had drawn an arrow extending downward.

"Olly was quite right," the professor said. "That aperture was never intended to be a source of sunlight. I think it has an entirely different function. And if I'm right, it's one that doesn't reveal itself until after the moon has set."

"It's for moonlight!" Josh gasped.

The professor laughed. "Exactly!" he confirmed. "The parchment contains a section that refers to the full moon. We all just assumed it was a reference to the talisman, but I think it means much more than that. If I'm right, then the hole in the roof of the shrine was cut to allow the light of the full moon in."

Jonathan stared at the drawing. "So when the full moon is in exactly the right place in the sky," he said slowly, "it will shine down onto a particular point in the shrine."

"What do you think it will shine on?" Olly's grandmother asked.

"The place where the talisman is hidden, of course!" Olly exclaimed.

"We can't be sure of that until we test my theory out," said her father. "But it must illuminate something important for them to have cut through so much rock."

Josh looked up at the night sky. "It will be a full moon tomorrow night," he said.

"Indeed it will," agreed Professor Christie. "I think we should arrange with our colleagues that we all take a trip up to the Temple of Ganesha tomorrow night, and then we'll see where the moonlight falls."

"A night in the temple," Olly breathed. "That will be so cool."

"I don't think you and Josh will be able to go," put in Mrs. Beckmann.

Josh and Olly both stared at her in horror.

"But we have to!" Olly exclaimed. "They can't do it without us."

"Listen, you two," Mrs. Beckmann said quite kindly. "If it was just Jonathan and the professor, then I'm sure some room could be found for you. But the others will be going up there, too, and I doubt they will be as tolerant as the professor is about having young people underfoot. I'm afraid you'll have to sit this one out. I'm sorry."

"But, Gran!" Olly wailed.

Her grandmother raised a silencing finger. "If anything is found, you'll learn all about it first thing in the morning," she said firmly.

Olly didn't bother arguing with her grandmother right then, but she planned on having plenty to say about it before the following night. Only over her dead body would she let the archaeologists head up to the temple and find the Elephant of Parvati without her!

~~~~~

Olly managed to have a chat with Josh after the meal, before they went to bed. They sat on Olly's bed in her room and whispered softly together.

"If the professor is right," Josh said, "it wrecks our theory about a hidden temple near Elephant Falls."

115

"I'm not so sure," Olly replied. She had been doing some thinking, and she had come up with a theory of her own. "What if he's right about the hole letting in moonlight, but what if the moonlight doesn't fall exactly on the place where the talisman is hidden?"

Josh looked puzzled. "I don't understand."

"Do you remember what the inside of the shrine looks like?" Olly asked. "Parvati is standing on a kind of cliff, isn't she? And the water runs over the edge of the cliff and pours down into the bowl. Now, does that remind you of anything? Maybe something like a *real* waterfall?"

Josh looked at her. "You mean Elephant Falls," he said.

Olly nodded. "*Parvati* Falls," she corrected him. "What if the waterfall in the shrine is meant to represent Parvati Falls?"

"Like a kind of model, you mean?" Josh asked. "A three-D map?" His eyes widened with excitement. "So the moonlight wouldn't be shining down on the actual hiding place of the talisman — it would just show you where to look on the *real* waterfall. Olly, we have to tell Jonathan and the professor!"

Olly shook her head. "I don't think we should do

that," she whispered. "They'll just go off and tell Ethan. They'll feel like they have to since Ethan organized this whole thing. Then all Ethan has to do is wait for the moonlight to show him where to dig. And before we know it, he'll have found the hidden temple and the talisman."

Josh frowned. "You're right," he agreed. "But even if we don't say anything, the professor's bound to work out what the moonlight is really showing." He sighed heavily. "So, Ethan's going to win either way."

"Not necessarily," Olly said. "If the waterfall in the shrine is a copy of Parvati Falls, then maybe whatever happens in the shrine will also happen at the real falls. Isn't that possible?"

Josh looked dubious. "I guess so," he said. "But that hole was carved in the temple to let just a thin beam of moonlight shine through and pinpoint one spot. The moon won't have the same effect out in the open, will it?"

"Maybe not," Olly replied. "But there's one good way to find out."

Josh raised his eyebrows. "You mean, you want to go up there?"

Olly nodded. "Tomorrow night," she told him. "After dinner, we wave good-bye to Dad and the others, putter around for a while — play a game of

Monopoly or something with Gran — and then pretend to go to bed as normal."

"And then we slip out while no one is looking," Josh continued, "and head toward Elephant Falls."

"Where we see something utterly marvelous and unbelievable," Olly finished. "Which leads us to the Elephant of Parvati! What do you think?"

Josh grinned at her. "I think it's crazy," he said. "But it's our only chance. Let's do it!"

~~~~~

It was the following day and their schoolwork was finally over. Mrs. Beckmann had gone to sit on the veranda, with a tall cool drink and a newspaper. Olly and Josh sat huddled together in Josh's room, planning out what they intended to say for Ethan Cain's benefit.

Looking at maps the day before had served them well. They had found the perfect place to send Ethan: an abandoned village called Gamsali in a nasty, swampy area, thirty miles to the east.

"Remember, you have to sound really convincing," Olly told Josh. "If he thinks you're faking, he won't fall for it."

Josh looked at her. "One of us has a mother who is a famous actress, right?" he demanded.

"Yeah," Olly replied.

"Don't worry about my acting talent," Josh said. "I've got this under control."

Olly stood up. "OK, then — let's go and win some Oscars!"

Josh walked to the door of the sitting room and grasped the handle. "Scene one, take one," he whispered. "Our intrepid heroes enter the room."

Olly rolled her eyes.

∿∿∿

"Dad still thinks the talisman is probably hidden somewhere in the Temple of Ganesha," Olly said as they walked into the room. "But if what Adhita Ram has just told us is true, then the Elephant of Parvati isn't anywhere *near* that temple." Olly and Josh sat down at the table.

"Yes, but yesterday he told us that there might have been a hidden temple by Elephant Falls," Josh pointed out. "So why should we believe him now, when he says he thinks the hidden temple is over at Gamsali? It's at least twenty-five miles away from here."

"He told us about the possibility of a temple near the falls before he realized what the rest of the parchment meant," Olly replied. "Most of the writing on the parchment is a list of directions for how to get *from* the waterfall to the place where the talisman was hidden. He's absolutely convinced that the Elephant of Parvati is in a lost temple over at Gamsali."

"Then I suppose we should tell Jonathan and the professor all about it," Josh suggested.

Olly smiled — now for the really brilliant part of their scheme. "I don't think we should tell them right away," she argued. "They'll only tell Ethan — and we don't want him to know about it before we've had time to do some double-checking." She managed to sound totally convincing; Josh gave her the thumbs-up as she continued. "I don't know how, but Ethan has been ahead of us all along. Now we know something he can't possibly have found out. I think we should ask Gran to take us for a ride tomorrow. We can get her to drive over to Gamsali, and once we're there, we can take a look around."

"Great idea," Josh agreed. "Adhita Ram said the temple was in the hills about three miles southeast of the town. It should be easy enough to find it with those directions."

"And when we do, we'll have beaten Ethan again!" Olly declared triumphantly.

"Are you hungry?" Josh asked, signaling that their little act was over.

"Yes, I am," Olly said. "Let's go and eat."

They left the room. Outside in the hall, Olly turned to Josh. "Do you think we were convincing?" she whispered.

Josh nodded. "I think we were brilliant," he replied. "We might make it as movie stars after all."

"I'll be an archaeologist–movie star," Olly said thoughtfully. "I don't think there are many of those around." She laughed. "Now we have to keep our fingers crossed that Ethan takes the bait."

"Oh, he will," Josh said. "Just you wait and see."

The two friends didn't have to wait very long to see that their little act had done the trick. About half an hour later, they were sitting on the front steps of the palace, chatting with Salila, when they saw Ethan Cain leave the hotel in a rented jeep.

Olly nudged Josh. Ethan was taking the road to the east — the road that led to Gamsali.

The friends grinned as they watched the jeep disappear.

"Why do you smile?" Salila asked.

"Our friend Ethan is going on a day trip to Gamsali," Olly began.

Salila frowned. "But there is nothing there," she said. "The village has been abandoned for years. Why would he go there?"

Olly and Josh looked at each other. "I think we may have given him the impression that there's something interesting there," Josh said with a grin.

Salila shook her head. "All he will find is an unpleasant swamp and a lot of hungry mosquitoes."

Olly laughed. "Great!" she said. "This just keeps getting better and better."

"We're playing a kind of practical joke on Ethan," Josh explained to Salila. "Trust me — he deserves it!"

Chapter Eleven: 🌙
Breaking and Entering

"Do you know what would be even better than Ethan getting stuck in a swamp and bitten half to death by bloodthirsty mosquitoes?" Olly asked.

"No," Josh replied. "What?"

They were stretched on lounge chairs on the hotel veranda, sipping cold drinks and soaking up some afternoon sunshine.

Olly sat up and peered at Josh over her sunglasses. "If we could prove to everyone what he's *really* like," she said.

Josh looked at Olly curiously. "And how would we do that?" he asked.

"Well," Olly began. "Why won't anyone believe that Ethan is a creep?"

"Because he always charms everyone into thinking he's innocent," Josh replied. "And because there's never any proof."

"Exactly!" Olly agreed. "But this time we *do* have some proof. We have the bug!"

Josh sat up. Olly had a good point. Ethan Cain

had always managed to sweet-talk his way out of trouble in the past, but what if they produced the hidden microphone in front of everyone?

"But how could we prove he planted the thing?" Josh asked, suddenly seeing the big flaw in Olly's idea. "You know what he's like. He'll act as shocked as everyone else when he sees the bug, and they'll all believe he didn't know anything about it."

"Rats!" Olly hissed, throwing herself back on the lounge chair. "You're right. Of course he will."

"Wait a minute, though," Josh said. "If he's been listening in on everything we've said, then he must have some kind of a receiver hidden in his suite."

A slow grin spread over Olly's face. "So, we tell everyone about the bug, march them all up to Ethan's suite, show them the receiver, and — *wham!* — he's busted! I like it, Josh. I really like it."

Josh shook his head. "They'd never agree to search his suite," he said. "The only way it'll work is if we can tell them exactly where the receiver is."

"Then, we have to find the receiver first," Olly said. She chewed her bottom lip thoughtfully. "How long do you think it'll take Ethan to get to the swamp and back?"

"A couple of hours, at least," Josh responded.

Olly clambered up off the lounge chair. "So that

means we've got about forty-five minutes left. Josh, what are you loafing around for? We've got some breaking and entering to do!"

~~~~~

The opulent Maharajah's Suite took up most of the top floor of the hotel. The corridor outside seemed deserted as Olly and Josh made their way stealthily across the thick carpet toward the grand doorway.

There was a brass plaque attached to the wall. It said: *The Maharajah's Suite. Designed by Buland Darza for his son, Akbar, in the year 1647.*

"It must be nice to have a dad who can afford to build you a place like this," Olly said quietly.

"It didn't do him much good," Josh reminded her. "Akbar died before he even moved in."

The friends stood before the door and stared at the heavy brass lock.

Josh glanced around at Olly. "How are we going to get in?" he asked.

"We could call room service," Olly suggested. "We could pretend we're calling from inside the suite and order something to eat. The waiters will have pass keys. When they come up to deliver the food, we'll slip in while they're not looking."

Josh stared at her. "That's ridiculous," he said.

"If a waiter comes up here and knocks on the door but doesn't get an answer, he'll just go down and tell management there's something funny going on. Then they'll send security people up to check it out."

Olly glared at him. "You come up with a better plan, then."

"There must be an unlocked door somewhere on this floor," Josh said. "We could go into that room and out onto the balcony. Then we could climb across to one of the Maharajah's Suite's balconies and go in the window."

"Or we could fall off the balcony and go splat on the ground!" Olly pointed out. "Which is a whole lot more likely, if you ask me." She stared at the door. "And we assume it's actually locked, right?"

Josh gave a scoffing laugh. "Of course it is!" he said. "Do you think Ethan is the kind of person to wander off without locking up behind him?"

"All the same," Olly insisted. "We should check."

"Really, Olly, how did you get so stubborn?" Josh said, stepping up to the door. He grasped the handle, turned it, and leaned against the door. It swung smoothly inward and Josh promptly fell through the doorway and landed flat on his face.

Olly crouched down beside him. "Are you OK?"

"Yes," Josh groaned. "I'm fine."

"Good. Then stop messing around and get up."

Josh clambered to his feet and looked around.

They were in a large room with deep blue curtains framing ornate latticework windows. The ceiling was decorated with more gold, and a rich, thick carpet covered the floor. The furniture was lavish and obviously antique.

"I told you it was fancy up here," Josh murmured.

"OK, let's start searching," Olly said. "What exactly does a receiver look like?"

"In the movies, they're like big reel-to-reel tape recorders," Josh replied. "But it's more likely to be a small digital device. It might even be a computer. It's possible Ethan's got a laptop with the right software on it to act as a receiver."

Olly stared at him in confusion.

"Basically, anything electronic," Josh said. He pointed
to the left. "You go that way. I'll look over here."

Olly headed for the huge, mahogany desk by the balcony doors. None of the drawers were locked, but none contained anything suspicious. She did find one interesting thing, though. In the top, right-hand drawer there was a small black box. She opened it to see the silver key that they had found in the pottery elephant.

She considered taking the key, but quickly realized that it wouldn't be a good idea. Ethan would be sure to notice that it was missing, and the last thing she wanted to do was put him on the alert.

She closed the drawer again and looked around. There was a large old cabinet by a set of double doors. Quickly, she moved over to search it. It was full of exquisite, old china and sparkling wineglasses, but no laptop and no electronics of any kind.

Olly opened the double doors and went through into another large, luxurious room. The furniture was very grand, with long couches, deep armchairs, and small round tables holding statues of the Hindu gods.

The golden afternoon sunlight streamed in through the tall windows, giving the room an otherworldly look, and making Olly feel as if she was walking through an ancient Indian fable. She imagined herself as the daughter of a wealthy Maharajah from hundreds of years past. She'd be dressed in silks and satins, with scores of servants at her beck and call. She walked regally toward the next door, smiling to herself.

She was just reaching for the door handle when the door swung open and she found herself staring into the startled eyes of Ethan Cain's personal assistant.

Olly let out a squawk. It had never occurred to her that there might be someone in the suite. But clearly there was, and now she was caught!

Paul glared at her with narrowed eyes. "What are you doing in here?" he snapped, stepping into the room and closing the door behind him.

The thought sped through Olly's mind: *It's in there! The receiver is in there!* But she couldn't think what to say. "Well, the thing is . . ." she began, racking her brains for a plausible excuse.

"We were just exploring," came Josh's voice from behind her. "The door was open; we didn't think Ethan would mind."

Olly glanced over her shoulder. He must have heard her stifled yell and come running, she realized. *Good for Josh!* "That's right," Olly said, picking up on Josh's lead. "I'm sure Ethan wouldn't mind us looking around. It's amazing up here. Prince Akbar would have loved it if he hadn't been killed before he could move in." She smiled her most innocent smile. "Isn't that a shame?" she went on. "His father must have been really upset." She walked over to an old chest and ran her hand over the carved wood. "Do you know how old this is? Would it have been here at the time — or maybe it was added later. What do you think?"

Paul stared at her, confusion mixed with anger on his face. "I'm afraid I really don't know," he answered. "But you shouldn't be in here without Mr. Cain's express permission."

Olly gave him an innocent look. "Why's that?" she said cheerfully. "Has he got something to hide?"

Her attitude seemed to take him aback. "That's not the point," Paul said sharply. "Mr. Cain doesn't allow anyone to come in here without his permission."

Olly could tell he was annoyed, but he was doing his best to keep it under control. After all, Josh was the son of his boss's girlfriend.

"Oh, well, if that's the case," Josh said calmly, "I guess we'd better be leaving."

Olly nodded. "Yes — sorry to have bothered you," she added.

Mr. White looked hard into her face, but she just smiled back at him.

"I'm sure Mr. Cain will be only too happy to give you a tour of the suite," Paul said, clearly doing his best to remain polite. "But please ask next time."

"Will do," Olly said as she and Josh headed for the door.

Paul followed them all the way.

"Bye, now," Olly said. "Have a nice day."

Paul closed the door behind them and they heard the sharp scrape of the key turning in the lock.

Josh put his finger to his lips and gestured that they should get out of earshot.

"Oh! He almost scared me to death!" Olly said once they were a safe distance away. "Do you think he suspected anything?"

"I don't know," Josh replied. "But he's bound to tell Ethan — and there's no way Ethan is going to believe we were just up there to have a look around. He knows us too well for that."

They made their way down the stairs and out into the gardens.

"I don't suppose you had time to find anything interesting, did you?" Olly asked hopefully as they sat on the edge of one of the fish ponds.

"Not a thing," Josh sighed.

"I bet the receiver was in that room Paul came out of," Olly said. "What do you think Ethan will do when he hears we were up there?"

"Whatever he does, we've blown our only chance of finding out where the receiver is," Josh said. "And that was our only proof that he's been listening in on us."

"We still have the bug," Olly pointed out. "If we show that to Dad and Gran — and tell them that we're absolutely certain Ethan planted it — we *might* be able to convince them."

Josh's eyes brightened. "At the very least, they'll want to set up an investigation. They might even call in the police," he said thoughtfully. "And then, with any luck, there might be some clues that will lead back to Ethan."

"It's worth a try," Olly declared, jumping up. "Dad and Jonathan are in another of those meetings, but Gran should be around somewhere. Let's go and get the bug and show it to her."

They ran up to their suite. As they turned into the hallway, they saw someone slip quietly around the corner at the far end.

"Who was that?" Olly asked.

"I don't know," Josh answered.

"It looked like Paul White," Olly said. She stared at Josh. "What's he doing here?" A horrible thought flashed across her mind. She rushed to the doors of the suite and threw them open. Then she ran across the carpet and ducked under the table, peering up at the underside of the tabletop.

Olly let out a yell of frustration. Her suspicions had proved right: The bug was gone.

Chapter Twelve:
Peril by Moonlight

The late afternoon sun was throwing long shadows as Olly and Josh sat at a table in a quiet corner of the long veranda that ran along the front of the hotel. The disappearance of the bug was a real blow, made all the worse by the fact that they felt they should have seen it coming.

"I can guess exactly what happened after Mr. White got rid of us," Josh said. "He got right on his cell phone to tell Ethan all about it. And Ethan guessed why we were up there."

"And told him to go down to our suite and take the bug away," Olly sighed.

Josh's face brightened. "At least one good thing's come out of it," he said. "Ethan can't listen in on us anymore."

Olly nodded. "And we did manage to send him off into a nasty swamp, looking for a nonexistent temple," she added with a smile. "So, the day hasn't been a complete disaster." She chuckled. "He's not going to be a very happy bunny when he gets back."

As if in response to her words, a jeep came roaring up to the front of the hotel in a cloud of dust. One of the hotel porters ran down the steps to open the car door.

Ethan Cain emerged, looking disheveled and furious. He said something to the porter, who climbed into the jeep and drove it around to the parking area at the side of the hotel.

His face thunderous, Ethan stalked up the steps to the veranda. Olly watched him with a cheerful smile on her face.

As soon as Ethan caught sight of Olly and Josh, his face miraculously cleared. He took a moment to straighten his clothes and smooth his hair and then strode toward them with a wide smile on his face.

"Have you been anywhere interesting?" Josh asked innocently.

"Oh, here and there, you know," Ethan replied, leaning on the back of a chair. "We have to follow up on all kinds of leads. Some of them are useful, and others are kind of a waste of time."

Olly watched his face. She had to admit that he was a great actor. There wasn't a glimmer of anger in his expression now.

"It must be annoying when you think you're onto

something big, but it turns out to be a miserable swamp," she said.

A gleam came into Ethan's eye. "What makes you mention a swamp, Olly?" he asked.

She pointed to his mud-caked boots and trousers. "You look like you've been in a swamp, that's all," she said. "Was it nasty?"

"It was a little uncomfortable," Ethan admitted. "But I learned something really interesting while I was there." He smiled from Olly to Josh. "And I figured something out, too — so it wasn't a complete waste of time."

"What did you figure out?" Josh asked.

Ethan smiled. "Oh, I just put one and one together and made two," he told them. "By the way, Paul called. He said you were having a look around my rooms." Olly opened her mouth to speak, but Ethan raised a hand to silence her. "I don't mind at all," he went on. "It would be more polite of you to ask first, that's all. Oh, and any time you'd like another look around, just let me know and I'll be happy to give you a guided tour — in case there's anything up there that you missed." He straightened up. "And now, I think I'd better freshen up; I've got work to do this evening."

"I suppose you'll be going up to the Temple of Ganesha with the others?" Olly inquired.

Ethan smiled. "Actually, no, I'm going to have to miss that," he said. "I'm sure your father will be able to deal with anything they might find up there. I've got some other business to deal with." He turned and walked toward the entrance of the hotel. "In fact, if my business tonight works out, I'm expecting to have some really big news for everyone in the morning," he called back. "Catch you guys later."

Olly and Josh looked at each other as the amateur archaeologist disappeared into the hotel.

"What do you think he meant by that?" Olly asked.

"Beats me," Josh replied, frowning.

"I don't like the sound of it," Olly said. "He has contacts all over this area. What if he's been told something we don't know about? Something about the hidden temple?"

"Well, if he has, there's nothing we can do about it," Josh sighed. "We should stick to our plan and go up to Elephant Falls. Let's just keep our fingers crossed that something exciting happens up there tonight." He lowered his voice. "Because otherwise I've got a bad feeling that Ethan is going to get to the Elephant of Parvati first!"

Olly and Josh stood on their balcony, watching as the small convoy of jeeps wound its way up the road toward the Temple of Ganesha. Every one of the professors and doctors had wanted to be there to see if Professor Christie's theory was correct. Ben Wilder had also come up from Tauri to record the whole adventure.

It seemed that, apart from the hotel staff and Olly's grandmother, the whole of the Peshwar Palace was deserted.

Josh watched the jeeps move up into the night-dark hills, the beams of their headlights gradually fading away in the darkness. There was a knot of excitement in his stomach at the thought of his own plans for the evening. He knew Mrs. Beckmann would be livid if she found out that he and Olly had left the hotel without her permission. But, as Olly had pointed out, if they found the talisman all would be forgiven. And if they found nothing, they would just creep back to the hotel and no one would be any the wiser.

The friends turned away from the night and walked back into the sitting room. Olly's grandmother was seated in an armchair, reading her book.

"They've gone," Olly said, flopping down onto the couch. "Some people get all the fun."

Her grandmother looked up. "I hope you're not going to mope around the place all evening," she said.

Olly gave her a smile. "No, Josh and I are going to play some games on Jonathan's laptop," she replied. Then she yawned and stretched. "Although I think I might need an early night, tonight. I'm exhausted." She looked at her grandmother. "How about you? Are you feeling sleepy at all?"

Mrs. Beckmann glanced at her wristwatch. "It's only five past eight," she remarked, looking rather surprised.

"Come on," Josh declared, grabbing Olly and hustling her out of the room before she could say anything else. "We'll set the computer up in my room."

He closed the door between them and Mrs. Beckmann. "Really subtle, Olly," he hissed. "Why don't you make it even more obvious that you want her out of the way? You just need to be patient for a while!"

Olly threw herself down on the bed. "Yes, yes," she said. "I'm great at being patient!"

Josh grinned at her as he opened the laptop and

booted it up. He had a feeling it was going to be a long, long evening.

~~~~~

Josh lay in bed listening to Mrs. Beckmann's footsteps in the living room. He looked at his watch. The luminous dial glowed in the darkness; it was almost eleven o'clock. He sat up, listening intently and staring at the thin line of light under his door. Suddenly, the light went out. A moment later, there was the click of a door closing — and then silence.

Josh slipped out of bed. He was fully clothed except for his shoes. He tiptoed to the door and put his ear to the wooden panels. There wasn't a sound from the sitting room: Mrs. Beckmann had finally gone to bed.

He found his shoes in the dark and put them on. He was just tying the laces when his bedroom door opened and a shadow slipped inside.

"I thought she was going to stay up all night," Olly whispered. "I've brought a flashlight with me. Are you ready?"

"Yes," Josh whispered back. "But I've been thinking. We've forgotten all about the key. If we find the hidden temple and manage to get inside, we might need it."

"Ethan probably has the copy that he had made," Olly said. "But the original is up in his desk. I saw it. It's in a little black box in the top right-hand drawer."

"Perfect!" Josh said. "Then we should go and get it."

"What if we get caught in Ethan's suite again?" Olly asked.

"It's worth the risk," Josh replied. "We need to have that silver key."

〰〰

The door to the Maharajah's Suite was locked this time.

"I know how we can get in," Josh whispered as they stood in the corridor. "I know you thought it was a stupid idea last time I mentioned it, but when we were down on the veranda earlier I noticed that all the balconies on the top floor are linked together. We can do what I suggested: Go into another room and climb across."

They found an unlocked door farther along the corridor. It was a small room that was being used for storage and it didn't have a balcony. But the window had a wide ledge, and it was only a single long step from there to the main balcony of the Maharajah's Suite.

"I'll climb out and go in through the balcony doors," Josh said, eyeing the gap uneasily. "You wait by the main door — I'll come and open it for you."

"Be careful," Olly warned.

Josh nodded. He climbed onto the windowsill, and keeping a tight hold on the masonry, got gradually to his feet. A cool breeze drifted over his face. Even in the darkness, he was well aware of the long drop to the paving stones below.

He turned so that he was facing the wall. It was only a few feet to the edge of the balcony. He clung to the stonework and carefully extended a foot. Once he had a firm footing, he reached out an arm, gripped the top of the balcony, and started to swing himself across.

But his shoe slipped on the stone and for a moment Josh found himself hanging by his arms, his feet dangling in midair. Olly squawked in alarm, but then Josh regained his footing and quickly threw himself over the banister. He lay panting on the floor of the balcony, praying that the doors onto it were unlocked — he didn't want to have to go back the way he had come.

Eventually, Josh got to his feet and tried the doors. To his relief, they swung open easily. He crept into the room, carefully closing the doors behind him. The place was in darkness, but a sliver of light under an adjacent door showed that someone was still awake. Josh swallowed hard — he knew he would need to be quick and silent.

The big desk was in front of him. He tiptoed to the top right-hand drawer and slid it quietly open, wincing at the soft scrape of wood on wood. He paused, for a moment, listening for any sign that he had been overheard. But all he could hear was the roar of his own blood surging through his temples. He inched the drawer farther open — there was the black box, just as Olly had described it. Josh lifted the lid. The little silver key was still there, gleaming in the moonlight. Quickly, Josh picked it up and slipped it into his pocket.

Smiling, he closed the drawer again and padded over to the main door of the suite. The key was in the lock. He turned it and started to push the door open. But, suddenly, the door swung inward toward Josh, and Olly came tumbling into the room.

She closed the door behind her. "I heard the elevator — there's someone coming," she hissed, her voice a sharp whisper in the gloom.

"Who?" Josh breathed.

"I don't know." Olly pressed her ear to the door. "I can hear the elevator doors opening now."

A few moments later, there was a sharp rap on the door and a voice called out, "Room service!"

"I'm coming!" answered a voice from the adjoining room where the light was on.

Josh and Olly exchanged a look. They had both recognized the voice as Paul White's. They heard Paul get up and head toward the main room to answer the door.

Josh looked at Olly in despair — they were trapped.

Chapter Thirteen: The Moonlit Veil

It was Olly who saved them from discovery. She dived for cover down by the side of a large, old cabinet, pulling Josh along with her. A split second later the lights came on and they heard footsteps crossing the room.

They stared at each other, hardly daring to breathe, as Paul approached. They heard him turn the key in the lock and try to open the door.

Olly groaned inwardly. Josh had unlocked it — which meant that Paul had locked it again when he thought he was *un*locking it. He would only need to put two and two together to realize that something strange was going on.

"It's room service, sir," came the voice from outside. "I have the food you ordered."

"Wait a moment," Paul replied, wrestling with the door.

They heard him turn the key again, and grunt with surprise as the door opened.

Paul spoke briefly with the man outside and then

they heard the door close again. Olly waited breath-lessly for the footsteps to move back across the floor — but there was a tense silence in the room. Ever so carefully, she peeped past the corner of the cabinet to try and see what was going on.

Paul was standing with his back to the door and a silver tray in his hands, frowning in thought. After a moment, he shrugged, turned back to the door, and twisted the key in the lock. For one dread-ful second, Olly thought he might take the key with him, but he didn't. He headed back to the room he had come from, switched the light off in the main room, and closed the door behind him.

Olly let out a long sigh of relief. "That was close!" she said.

"I've got the silver key," Josh whispered. "Let's get out of here."

Olly led the way across the room, turned the key, and eased the door open. She and Josh slipped out and Olly silently closed the door again.

Josh took the silver key out of his pocket and held it up for Olly to see.

"Great," she said. "Now, let's go to Elephant Falls!"

〰〰〰

It took them an hour or more to make their way to Elephant Falls. They used the shortcut that Salila had shown them, up and down the rolling hills and in and out through the forests in the bright moonlight. Even under the canopy of the trees they could still see quite clearly. The full moon was huge in a sky teeming with stars. Its light cast shadows that seemed to dance mysteriously around them.

The waterfall was fabulously beautiful in the silvery light — the endless cascade of water glinting and sparkling, the rising mist like a silver cloak around the shoulders of the hills. The lake itself shimmered and gleamed like liquid silver in the starlight.

"Oh, wow!" Olly breathed as she gazed at the moonlit falls. "It was worth coming here just to see this."

"It is pretty amazing," Josh agreed. He walked on down to the edge of the lake, while Olly stood staring at the spectacle of Elephant Falls.

"You coming or what?" Josh called, after a moment.

"I'm coming," Olly replied, and took one last look at the waterfall in all its moonlit splendor. She was just about to run down and join Josh by the lake, when something caught her eye. As she stared at the waterfall, she thought she could glimpse something in the curtain of water. It was a shape —

visible one moment, gone the next. She stared for a few moments more but the shape seemed to have vanished.

"Olly, come on," shouted Josh.

Olly looked down at her friend, and as she glanced away from the waterfall, the curious shape caught the corner of her eye again. It looked like a silver arch in the water. But when she looked straight at it again, there was nothing there.

"Josh," she called. "Come back up here. I want you to look at something."

Josh clambered back up to where Olly was standing. "What is it?" he asked.

She pointed to the place where she had seen the phantom archway in the water. "Don't look straight at it," she told him. "Just focus your eyes to one side, and then tell me what you see."

Josh did as she instructed. "What am I looking for?" he inquired.

"I'm not going to tell you," Olly replied. "I want you to see it for yourself."

"This is dumb," Josh argued. "I can't see anything . . . Oh!" He stared hard at the waterfall. "That was weird."

Olly smiled. "What did you see?"

"It was like a kind of arch in the water," Josh

explained. "But I can't see it when I look directly at it. I suppose it must be some kind of optical illusion. There can't actually be anything in the waterfall, though, can there? It's just the way the moonlight is shining on the water."

"Do you remember what Adhita Ram said?" Olly breathed. "'To see beyond the moonlit veil, the seeker must look without looking.'"

Josh stared at her. "That's right," he said. His eyes widened. "It must mean the veil of the waterfall."

"And you can only see it if you don't look directly at it," Olly said. "Josh — I think the hidden temple is behind the waterfall!"

Josh stared at the rugged cliffs. "Is there a way up there?" he asked.

Olly pointed. "Yes," she said. "Look!" It wasn't obvious unless you were searching for it, but a rugged path did seem to wind its broken way along the cliff face toward the waterfall.

The two friends hurried around the lake, and up to the place where the path seemed to start. It led them up through the rocks beside the waterfall. They scrambled along as quickly as they could climb, sometimes side by side — helping each other over the tricky parts — sometimes in single file between boulders or clefts in the cliff.

Always, as they climbed, the silver moonlight shined down upon them and the roar of the water-fall echoed in their ears.

Olly clambered up a final steep slope and found herself standing on a precarious ledge. She helped Josh up beside her and the two of them stood there for a few moments, recovering from the climb.

Olly glanced back the way they had come. Bone-breaking rocks tumbled down some sixty feet into the valley below. Ahead, the path toward the water-fall rose and fell. Sometimes it was no more than the width of a cautiously placed foot, sometimes it was wide enough to walk along with comparative ease. It looked old and worn, and as if it might crumble away at any time, but Olly wasn't going to let that stop her.

She couldn't see the silver arch in the water any-more — but she was absolutely certain that it was there and that it would lead them to the hidden temple. She edged onward along the path, with Josh right behind her.

As they drew nearer to the falls, they felt fine spray on their hands and faces. The powerful tor-rent of water was only a few feet ahead of them now, waiting to sweep them off the narrow path and impale them on the jagged rocks below.

But the path ran *behind* the waterfall, and Olly found herself edging under an overhang of rock and along a ledge that echoed to the noise of the cascading water. It was impossible to converse, and almost impossible to think.

She glanced back at Josh. He was right behind her, his hair dark with spray, his face spangled with water droplets, and his eyes glowing in the strange silvery light.

Olly moved farther along the ledge behind the waterfall. The rock beneath her feet was slick with water, but it formed a smooth and level pathway — on one side, the sheer cliff face, on the other, the curtain of constantly falling water. And through the shining water, Olly could just make out the bright disc of the full moon.

Suddenly the pathway shot off to the right, tunneling its way deep into the cliff face. Here there was a beautiful archway of fine silverwork. Olly took out her flashlight and switched it on. The beam shined along the tunnel, and Olly let out a gasp of wonder and delight. At the end of the tunnel — about thirty feet away — the flashlight beam gleamed on a pair of tall silver gates.

Olly and Josh walked forward together and gazed at the exquisite gates. They were etched with an intricate design of blossoms and vines, with sculpted silver flowers and dancing figures. The gates were three or four times Olly's height as she stood underneath them, gazing upward in speechless amazement.

Olly thought about the little silver key — could such a very small thing have been used to lock such immense gates? She looked at the silver panels where the doors met — but she couldn't see a keyhole and there were no handles. So, how did the doors open? Before she had time to share this puzzle with Josh, he pushed against the doors.

Smoothly they swung open, allowing Olly and Josh to step, in rapt silence, into the hidden Temple of Parvati.

The light from Olly's flashlight revealed an awesome sight. The center of the chamber was dominated by a towering statue of Parvati. The beautiful goddess was seated cross-legged on a deep plinth of beaten silver. She was wearing a painted pink sari, edged with golden braid. There were gold, bejeweled bracelets on her arms and wrists. A golden belt gleamed at her waist and a necklace of pearls hung around her neck. On her head was a high golden crown, studded with jewels in all the colors of the rainbow. Her face was beautiful, smiling, and serene, and in her outstretched hands she held a carved wooden elephant.

As Olly approached the statue, other wonders were revealed in the beam of the flashlight. The walls and ceiling were entirely paneled in silver and gold, engraved with a multitude of figures that danced and fought, walked and talked, or sat in contemplative silence. The decorations were so lavish and so detailed that Olly could only take in a fraction of the designs revealed in the scattered flashlight beam.

Stone pillars supported the golden roof. They were painted in bright colors and decorated with inscriptions and carvings of lotus flowers and fruit.

Olly knew the temple must be very, very old, but she saw that somehow the colored paint had remained bright and vibrant. She guessed that it had been protected from the bleaching power of the sun by the darkness of the hidden cavern.

Behind her the tunnel echoed with the sound of the waterfall, but in the fabulous chamber it was possible for Olly and Josh to speak without shouting.

"I wonder how long this has been here," Josh said.

"A very long time," Olly replied, her eyes fixed on the polished wooden elephant that rested on the two enormous hands of Parvati. The carved elephant was about a foot and a half long from trunk to tail. It was unadorned and quite smooth, the natural grain of the wood showing up clearly in the flashlight beam.

"This must be the Elephant of Parvati!" Olly breathed, as she walked toward it. She handed Josh the flashlight and stepped up to the broad silver dais on which the statue sat. Parvati towered over Olly, her beautiful face high above Olly's head, but her outstretched hands just within reach.

"Be careful," Josh said, as Olly stretched up toward the wooden elephant. "It's probably really heavy."

"Yes," came another voice from the shadows. "Be very careful, Olly — I wouldn't want you to drop it."

Startled, Olly turned toward the familiar voice.

Ethan Cain stepped from a dark corner of the chamber and switched on his flashlight. He held up something between the fingers of his other hand, shining the flashlight on it so that Josh and Olly could see it clearly.

It was the copy of the silver key.

"I thought this might come in handy tonight," he said, smiling. "I see you have the original, Olly. I will have to have a stern word with Paul when I get back. He was supposed to be on guard."

Olly glared at Ethan, speechless with anger and dismay.

He stepped forward, his arms spread wide. "What? No questions?" he asked. "I thought you'd want to know how I got here first."

"I can work that out for myself, thanks," Olly told him, her voice cold with contempt. "You listened in on us, and then guessed the rest."

Ethan smiled. "Once I knew you'd found my little device, I realized that what Adhita Ram had told you about a hidden temple by Elephant Falls must be true," he said. "And so I came here while the others went to the Temple of Ganesha. And I saw the silver archway through the water — as I imagine you did, too." He smiled. "The moonlit veil! Very poetic." He looked at the wooden elephant. "I assume we're all thinking the same thing? That the talisman is inside the elephant? I had a few moments to look at it before I heard you coming — I think you'll find it opens up." He took another step forward. "Olly — be a friend and hand it down to me, will you?"

Olly glared at him and didn't move.

"Oh, come now," Ethan said. "Be fair. We both wanted the prize and we both used rather underhanded methods to get it. After all — you did send me off to that swamp this afternoon. Now that wasn't very fair, was it?"

"The only reason you're here is because you were listening in on everything *we* said," Josh put in. "We worked the whole thing out — you didn't do a thing."

Ethan's eyebrows rose. "Really?" he said. "But, Josh — it was one of my employees who found the parchment in the first place. And it was I who funded the conference and brought all those people together. And it was I who arranged for your room to be bugged." He spread his hands again. "And you tell me I didn't do anything? On the contrary" — his voice suddenly took on a sharp edge — "I did *everything*!"

"No," Olly said. "We worked it all out for you."

The American laughed. "That's right, Olly," he said. "Like puppets on strings — and *I* was pulling the strings."

Olly stared down at him in horror. The terrible thing was that he was right — he had set the whole thing up, and they had fallen into his trap, solved the mystery, and found the Elephant of Parvati for him.

"We'll tell Jonathan and the professor everything," Josh said. "We'll tell them all about the bug."

"You're welcome to do that if you wish." Ethan

laughed. "But do you really think anyone will even believe that there *was* a bug? Let alone that *I* planted it? I will be suitably horrified when you tell everyone about it. In fact, I'll organize a thorough investigation . . ."

Olly's heart sank because she knew Ethan was right. No one would believe that he had planted a bug in their suite. And as for finding the talisman — he could just say that he followed the trail of clues in exactly the same way that she and Josh had.

This time, it seemed he really had beaten them.

"Now then," Ethan snapped. "Give me the elephant, Olly. I can make life very uncomfortable for you if you don't." His eyes narrowed. "Who knows, with the right words whispered in the right ears, I might arrange it so you never get to travel with your father again," he continued. "How does life in a boarding school appeal to you, Olly? Exciting enough?"

Olly glared at Ethan Cain, too angry to reply. She turned and grasped hold of the elephant. Josh had been right — the wooden statue was very heavy. She could only just manage to lift it out of Parvati's hands.

But as she did so, something startling happened. The statue's hands rose sharply with a loud creak.

Olly staggered backward with the heavy wooden sculpture clasped to her chest.

Another strange sound began to reverberate around the chamber. A scraping sound, like stone rubbing heavily on stone. Ethan, Olly, and Josh stood transfixed as the strange noises echoed back and forth between the temple walls.

And then there was another sound: the harsh clang of metal striking metal. The silver gates had slammed shut.

Josh turned and ran to the gates. He tried to drag them open, but there were no handles. He tried to get his fingers between them, but the panels met seamlessly. He grasped at the projecting parts of the silver carvings and hauled on them with all his strength, but the gates would not move.

And now a new and far more frightening sound began to echo through the cavern. The sound of rushing water.

Ethan flicked his flashlight around the chamber. Long dark slots had opened up in the walls, and as Olly stared at them in alarm, great spouts of water came pouring out.

Ethan gave a howl of fear and ran to join Josh at the gates, but water swept his feet from under him and he vanished in the flood. Olly saw his flashlight glowing for a few moments through the water, then it was gone.

Josh pressed up against the gates as the water rose to his knees. He began to climb, but Olly could see that the water was rising with him, and threatening to pull him down again.

For a few moments, Olly found herself on an island amidst the flood. But then the rising water came lapping over the dais, cold and dark and deadly. She gazed around frantically, clutching the wooden elephant to her chest as the water began to rise up her legs.

The water level was rising swiftly and there was no way out of the chamber. Soon the flood had reached Olly's waist. She pressed herself against the statue of Parvati, as if hoping the goddess would somehow save her.

But then an undercurrent tugged at her feet and Olly fell, losing her grip on the elephant as her head plunged beneath the rushing water and everything went black.

Chapter Fourteen: Floodwater

Josh scrambled up the gates, his fingers and the toes of his shoes only just finding a hold on the ornate silverwork. But the deadly floodwater pursued him relentlessly, swirling around the gates, rising ever higher. Terrified, Josh grasped his flashlight and pointed it around the echoing chamber. He saw that water was still pouring in through the vents high in the walls.

When Olly had lifted the carved elephant out of Parvati's hands, it had triggered some ancient, protective mechanism that opened sluice gates to the river. Its intention was hideously clear: to drown anyone who attempted to take the wooden elephant from Parvati's keeping.

Josh was at the top of the gates and he could clearly see that there was nowhere else to climb to. The water level was still rising, and even if it stopped, there was no way to escape from the temple chamber now that the gates had shut.

Josh aimed the flashlight at the place where

he had last seen Olly, clinging to the goddess as the water swept around her. The statue was now shoulder-deep in water — but Olly was gone.

Josh gasped. "Olly!" he shouted over the thunder of the water. "Olly!"

Water dragged at his legs, trying to pluck him off his precarious perch on the gates. He shined the flashlight over the heaving surface of the water, desperate for some sign that Olly was still alive.

And then he saw something moving in the water. Somebody was splashing around, sending up white spray. It was Olly — still near to the statue of Parvati and trying to make her way back to the comparative safety of the statue's shoulders. But she was caught in the clashing currents of the flood.

Olly was a competent swimmer, but Josh knew he was better. Alone, she might not survive. With his help, he thought they might both make it to the statue. Josh didn't hesitate. He secured the cord of the flashlight around his wrist and then launched himself off his perch into the water. In the darkness, he could see nothing, but he knew which way to go. He struck out strongly for the statue and his friend.

When he reached Olly, he treaded water, holding the flashlight beam on her face.

She just had breath left to spit out a few words. "I'm OK, but I've lost the elephant."

"Don't worry about that now," Josh gasped. "Try to get back to the statue." She nodded and they began to swim together.

The water was breaking over Parvati's shoulders now — the temple was half-drowned and still the water was rising.

Josh made sure that Olly was secure on Parvati's left shoulder before swimming around to the other side and hauling himself up onto the right. He sat astride the ridge of stone, his legs dangling in the water, his arms clinging to the great head.

He heard Olly's voice over the roar of the water.

"Now what?" she shouted.

"Have you seen Ethan?" Josh yelled back.

Olly shook her head.

Slowly Josh scoured the surface of the rising tide with the flashlight beam. He had no wish to see Ethan drown, not if there was some chance of helping him. But there was no sign of him. Josh had the horrible, sickening feeling that Ethan might have drowned.

"Josh?" Olly called again. "Do you think we'll be able to stay afloat till the water stops rising?"

Josh aimed the flashlight at the high vents

through which the water was still pouring. Soon, the statue of Parvati would be covered by the rising water and there would be nothing for them to cling to. They would be able to keep their heads above the surface for a certain amount of time — treading water, helping each other. But for how long? Eventually their strength would run out, and if the water rose to completely fill the chamber, they'd drown in the temple for sure.

He summoned his courage, determined to keep Olly's spirits up, and called back to her. "We'll be fine," he told her. "The water can't rise much farther. Then we just need to hang on till it drains away." He hoped he sounded more convincing than he felt.

As he began to realize the hopelessness of their situation, Josh felt himself give way to despair. His head fell forward against the head of the goddess. And then he saw something that chased despair from his mind. He sat up and shined the flashlight on the side of Parvati's head. Within the intricately sculpted curves of Parvati's ear, he saw a small dark slot. A keyhole.

Adhita Ram's words came back to Josh: "When all is lost, turn the key in the lock in the ear." He and Olly had assumed that the parchment was referring

to an elephant's ear, or perhaps to Ganesha's ear —
but it looked like they had got it wrong. At least,
Josh *hoped* they had got it wrong.

He pushed his hand into his pocket and felt for
the silver key. Carefully, he pulled it out and slid it
into the hole. He gave a shout of triumph — the
key fitted perfectly.

"What's going on?" he heard Olly shout. But
Josh was too excited to respond.

He tried to turn the key. It resisted for a moment,
but then it turned smoothly in the lock. At first,
nothing seemed to happen, but then Josh felt a faint
shuddering from deep within the statue — as if age-
old mechanisms were shifting into gear. Then there
were deeper, louder sounds and the whole statue
started to vibrate.

"Josh!" Olly howled. "What's happening?"

"It's the silver key!" Josh yelled. "There's a keyhole in Parvati's ear, and the key fits! I think —"

But the rest of Josh's words were drowned out by
a cacophonous rumbling from all around the chamber. He stared at the walls — the vents were closing!
The flood of black water dwindled to a stream and
then a trickle, and then it stopped altogether.

A strange silence fell over the chamber.

"So the keyhole wasn't in an elephant's ear, after

all — it was in the statue of Parvati!" Olly cried. "Josh, you're brilliant." Her voice bubbled with relieved laughter. "We're saved!"

Josh leaned around the huge head to look at her. "We still have to get out of here," he pointed out.

Olly stared back at him, her hair clinging to her face in wet strands, her eyes shining. "Have you turned the key all the way?" she asked.

"I think so." Josh took hold of the key again and gave it another twist. As he pushed, the key suddenly clicked and twisted farther in the lock. This time, Josh could clearly hear mechanisms moving within the head of the statue, as the farther turn of the key set some new device in motion. There was a low grumbling from beneath the water, and then silence.

"What happened then?" Olly asked.

"I don't know," Josh replied slowly.

But then they heard a booming clang and saw the tall silver gates swing open. The trapped floodwater went streaming out of this new exit and Olly was swept away in the rush.

Josh saw the water drag her off the statue's shoulder, and he lunged forward to catch her. But Olly's weight only served to pull him away from the statue, too.

Josh felt himself dragged along in the flood of water. He tried to keep hold of Olly, but she slipped from his grip. And then his head went under the water and Josh had to concentrate all his energy on trying to find the surface again. The water swept him along, turning him over and over until he was utterly disoriented. His head broke the surface for a moment and he was vaguely aware of being carried back along the tunnel that had led him and Olly to the temple. But the next second, the force of the water dragged him under again.

He held his breath, his head pounding as he was tumbled in the flood. He expected to be dashed against rocks at any moment. But then he saw a kind of brightness through the water and felt himself falling in a powerful cascade. The flood had taken him over the waterfall!

The sensation of falling seemed to last forever. But then Josh felt himself plunge into more water. He struggled upward, toward light and air, and eventually broke the surface to find that he was in the lake at the foot of Elephant Falls. The thunder of the falling water threw spray into his face and threatened to force him back underwater. So Josh swam away from the waterfall itself as quickly as he could. As soon as he was out of immediate danger, he turned in the water to search for any sign of Olly. His flashlight was lost — but now there was the bright moonlight to help him search.

After a moment, he spotted her over on the other side of the falls, and she was clinging to something — a large round shape that seemed to be buoying her up in the water. Josh swam toward her.

As he got closer, he realized what it was that she was hanging on to — it was the carved wooden elephant, but it had split open on a hinge along the spine.

"It banged against me in the rush," Olly gasped. "I just grabbed hold of it. I think it saved me. But it broke open when we hit the lake."

"Let's get to dry ground," Josh said.

"Josh!" Olly shouted. "Look! I think that came out of the wooden elephant when it split open." She was pointing to a small, round white shape bobbing on the surface of the lake a few feet away. Curved and buoyant, it slowly moved out of the eddies, turning in circles as the current caught it and carried it down to where the river flowed out from the far end of the lake.

"Get to dry land," Josh said. "I'll find out what it is."

He headed toward the white object. Glancing

over his shoulder, he saw Olly heading for dry land. She was safe — now he could concentrate on the white thing. But as he drew closer, something else took his attention. Something terrible. It was a human figure, floating facedown in the water.

Forgetting the bobbing white object, Josh swam strongly toward the floating man. He had passed his life-saving exam two years before, but until now he hadn't had much need to use the techniques he'd been taught.

He treaded water, using all his strength to turn the limp form over. He couldn't tell whether Ethan was breathing or if he was alive, but there was no time to think about that now. Josh swam around behind him, lodged his hand under Ethan's chin, and then struck out landward.

It was a difficult journey, and Josh was already tired, but he refused to give up. If there was any chance that Ethan had survived, then Josh was going to save him. He became aware of a frantic splashing behind his head and looked back to see that Olly had waded out into the lake to help him.

Together, they managed to drag Ethan out of the water.

"Is he dead?" Olly asked, her voice trembling.

Gasping for breath, Josh knelt by Ethan's chest.

The man's face was pale in the moonlight and water trickled from his mouth and nose. Josh tried to remember what he had learned. He turned Ethan onto his front and knelt astride his waist, pushing down hard on his back. Water gushed from his mouth.

Josh pushed down again. There was more water and then a weak cough.

Josh looked at Olly. "He's alive!" he said. He climbed off and together they turned Ethan into the recovery position. He was breathing normally now and his pulse felt strong.

Josh pushed the wet hair out of his eyes. "I think he's going to be OK," he said.

Olly gave a gasp of relief. "I thought he was dead," she said in an undertone.

"Another minute or two and he would have been," Josh told her. He stood up, trembling all over.

Olly went over to the wooden elephant which lay at the lakeside. She bent over and closed it with a sharp snap. "Whatever that white thing was from inside here, it's gone now," she sighed.

Josh turned and stared out over the lake. "Not yet!" he cried, excitement rising in his voice. "Look!"

If it wasn't for the bright moonlight, they would never have seen the small white blob at the far end of the lake. It was moving swiftly with the water now, heading down to where the river followed its winding course through the hills.

"We might still be able to get it," he said. "Come on!"

"What about Ethan?" Olly asked.

"He'll be fine for a minute or two," Josh said. "We'll come back for him."

Side by side, they ran along the bank of the long lake. Every now and then the white thing would be lost among the waves — but each time Josh thought it had vanished for good, it would come bobbing back into sight.

The lake narrowed between steep hills, and the river flowed down over rocks, the water foaming white as it raced along. Josh was slightly in the lead as the two friends bounded from rock to rock, desperate to keep up with the white thing in the water.

Josh redoubled his efforts and managed to edge slightly ahead of it. He jumped out onto a large boulder that jutted into the river and dropped to his knees. For a moment the thing bobbed tantalizingly within reach. Josh made a grab for it, but he couldn't get a grip and it bobbed away to be swept on down the river.

Olly came racing up to him. "Did you get it?" she panted.

"No. Almost," he gasped.

She gave a cry of frustration and ran on past him. Only a few feet ahead, more boulders pushed out into the river.

"There!" Josh yelled, pointing. "See it?" The thing had been caught in a swirling eddy. It was spinning around in the lee of a large rock.

"I see it!" Olly shouted. She leaped onto the rock and lay down on her front. She reached out and her fingers touched the smooth white object, but it bobbed and drifted away from her.

"Careful!" Josh shouted, as Olly leaned perilously far out over the churning water.

Her fingertips touched it again, and this time she managed to ease it toward herself. A moment later, she had a firm grasp on it. She sat up, cradling the thing in her lap. "Got it!" she gasped, grinning up at Josh as he ran to join her.

Olly got to her feet and held the thing out in triumph.

It was a white pottery elephant, quite stylized with its head tucked in and its trunk curled up to one side. It was fat and round, smooth and shiny, and no more than seven inches long. The legs and other features were shaped in quite a rudimentary way. Seated high on the curve of the animal's trunk was a tiny shrew.

Olly turned it over, frowning. The shiny porcelain had no holes or slots in it. She looked at Josh. "There's no way of getting into it," she said. She gently shook the elephant. There was no sound from inside. She frowned. "I don't think there's anything in it."

Josh gently took it out of her hands and slowly examined every inch. She was right — there were no slots, hinges, or holes in the smooth surface of the elephant.

"What should we do?" Olly asked. "This can't be the Elephant of Parvati, can it? That was supposed to be made of gold and jewels."

"I don't know," Josh said. "It might be. We did find Parvati holding it. We should take it to the Temple of Ganesha. The professor, Jonathan, and the others should still be there."

Olly nodded and the two of them began to trek back up the river toward the lake.

"We should check on Ethan first," Josh said. "If he's conscious he might be able to come with us.

If not, we'll have to leave him here and send help when we get to the temple." He shivered. "I'm looking forward to getting into some dry clothes."

Olly trudged along beside him. "Who cares about clothes! Just think about what we've found, Josh! Maybe we haven't got the talisman yet — but we found the hidden temple!"

They arrived back at the lake. Josh frowned. He was sure they ought to be able to see Ethan by now. They weren't far from where they had left him.

As they got closer to the place where they had dragged the half-drowned man from the lake, they realized that he was gone.

"He must have recovered," Josh said, staring all around. "But why did he wander off?"

"There's something else," Olly pointed out. "Wherever he's gone, he's taken the wooden elephant with him."

She was right. Both Ethan Cain and the elephant were gone.

Chapter Fifteen: ☾
Cracking the Nutshell

It was a long trek through the hills to the Temple of Ganesha in the dark, but the excitement of their discovery kept Olly and Josh in high spirits, despite their wet clothes and exhaustion.

Finally, they came to a familiar stretch of roadway, winding upward between rocky cliffs. They ran up to the crest of the hill and found themselves looking down at the facade of the temple. The moonlight threw strange and eerie shadows, making it seem to Olly as if all the human and animal figures on the carved rock-face were watching and waiting for her and Josh.

The jeeps that had come up from the palace were parked outside, but there was no other sign of life. Everything was silent under the huge full moon.

"I guess they're still in there," Olly said. She was clutching the white elephant protectively to her chest. "Let's go and show them what we've found."

Her own voice broke the mystical spell of the

place and, together, she and Josh walked down the hill to the temple.

"Where do you think Ethan went?" Josh asked.

Olly shrugged. "I don't know and I don't care," she said. "He's alive, but he didn't get his thieving hands on this." She lifted the elephant in her two hands. "And that's all I care about."

"But what is it?" Josh wondered. "It doesn't have any markings on it — and it doesn't fit the description of the talisman."

"It must be important, or it wouldn't have been inside the wooden elephant," Olly replied thoughtfully. "Maybe there's something about it that we can't see in this light." She looked up at the full moon, riding high in the star-bright sky. "It has to be something to do with the talisman, Josh — perhaps it's another clue."

As they approached the entrance to the Temple of Ganesha, they began to hear voices from within. They walked in through the heavy wooden doors just as a single voice rose above the others.

They looked at each other — the voice belonged to Ethan Cain.

Josh put his finger to his lips and Olly nodded. Before they made their presence known, they needed to know what Ethan was up to now.

They waited in the shadow of the doorway. The archaeologists were gathered at the foot of the stairway in the main sanctum. Lanterns stood on the ground, throwing out a soft yellow light that filled the chamber with leaping shadows. Ethan Cain was standing on the top stair, holding the wooden elephant in his hands. At his back, Ganesha gazed out over the temple with calm, untroubled eyes. Ben Wilder stood halfway up the stairs, filming Ethan on a camcorder.

"Again, I wish to apologize for not keeping you all up to date with my private researches into the parchment," Ethan was saying. "But I wanted to make sure that I was heading in the right direction before I drew too much attention to my findings. That is why I decided to investigate Elephant Falls alone tonight. An elderly mahout from the local area was able to make translations of a few sections of the parchment. This led me to believe that there was a lost temple to Parvati near the waterfall now called Elephant Falls, but once known as Parvati Falls. And, ladies and gentlemen, I was right — as this extraordinary artifact proves." He held the wooden elephant up for the camcorder. "I have only had a brief chance to study it," he continued. "But it is obvious that it is constructed in two halves and that it can be opened. I have no doubt that there is something of great significance within."

Olly's eyes narrowed with anger — Ethan was playing to the crowd of archaeologists, and to the camcorder, and making out that the discovery of the hidden temple and the elephant had all been down to him. *Typical!* she thought. She turned to look at Josh.

"Boy, is he in for a surprise!" Josh whispered.

Olly nodded and turned back to watch Ethan's next move. He had rested the elephant on the top step of the platform, beside the statue of Ganesha, and was crouching at its side with the iron copy of the silver key. Jonathan stood beside him, holding the elephant steady, while Ethan searched for a keyhole that wasn't there. The others watched in fascinated silence. Olly saw her own father among them, as thrilled as any by the find.

"Here!" Ethan said eventually. "I was expecting a keyhole, but this wooden clasp seems to be holding it together." He pressed his fingers against the wooden carving. There was a sharp click and the two halves fell open in Jonathan's hands.

Professor Christie climbed the steps to look at the relic. He stooped for a moment and then straightened up. "I'm afraid it's empty," he said.

"I don't understand," Ethan said in the profound silence that followed this revelation. Olly could almost have hugged herself with delight at the dumbfounded expression on his face. She grinned — it was time for a dramatic entrance.

"I think you're looking for this!" Olly announced loudly. She stepped out of the shadows, holding the porcelain elephant high in her hands. Josh was at her side as the archaeologists murmured in astonishment and parted to let them through.

"Olivia?" her father said. "What on earth are you doing here?"

A poisonous look came and went very quickly in Ethan's eyes as he glared at Olly and Josh. For a split second he looked as if he wanted to pounce on Olly and tear the prize out of her hands. But he recovered himself very quickly. "As I was about to tell you," he said, standing up, "Olly and Josh were on the same track as I." He looked at Professor Christie. "I'm sure you'll forgive them for leaving the hotel without permission, when you hear how helpful they were to me in locating the hidden Temple of Parvati." A smile spread across his face. "In fact, they saved me from drowning. They're a couple of heroes!"

"What have you got there, Olly?" Jonathan asked.

"Well, the temple filled with water when I took the wooden elephant out of Parvati's hands," Olly explained. "But Josh found the keyhole for the silver key, and all the water flooded out. We ended up in the lake at the bottom of the waterfall. The wooden elephant broke open." She nodded to the porcelain elephant in her hands. "And this was inside. We had to chase it down the river to catch up with it." Olly saw that Ben Wilder had turned the camcorder toward her and Josh. This wonderful moment was being captured on film! No matter what lies Ethan Cain told, no matter how he twisted the truth — she and Josh were the ones presenting this artifact to the world.

Almost giddy with pride and excitement, Olly ran up the stairs toward her father. But she missed her footing and stumbled on the stone steps. Her first instinct was to protect the porcelain elephant. She twisted, trying to fall onto her side. But her elbow slammed against the stone, and the elephant was jolted from her grasp.

She let out a cry of dismay as the elephant hit the step with a loud crack. But it didn't break. It rolled over the edge and struck the second step, still rolling. Olly watched, frozen in horror as the thing rolled and bounced down the stairs.

Josh lunged forward, trying to catch the tumbling elephant as it fell, but he moved a moment too late. The elephant rolled off the final step and struck the stone floor. This last impact was too much for the porcelain and it shattered into a hundred pieces.

Olly was too stunned even to cry out. She couldn't believe that this had happened. She had dropped the elephant that was the final clue to the whereabouts of the Elephant of Parvati, and now it lay in pieces. And, even worse, Ben Wilder had caught the whole humiliating, horrifying incident on film!

Olly put her head in her hands and groaned in absolute despair. When she looked up again, Josh was kneeling beside the broken relic, looking as wretched as her. But then something seemed to catch his eye and his expression changed. He leaned forward, spreading the porcelain fragments with his fingers, and picked up something, which he held out to Olly.

She stared at it in disbelief as it sparkled and flashed in the warm lantern light. It gleamed with gold and glittered with a thousand points of colored light.

Her despair and embarrassment forgotten, Olly got to her feet and walked slowly down the steps toward this wonderful shiny object. Josh laid it reverently in her hands and now Olly could see it properly.

It was a golden elephant, the size of Olly's hand. Hundreds of jewels adorned the elephant, making it sparkle and gleam with all the colors of the rainbow. It was beautiful beyond words.

Olly turned, holding the elephant up toward her father, speechless with joy.

She and Josh had found the Elephant of Parvati.

~~~~~

It was the evening following the dramatic discovery of the fourth Talisman of the Moon. Olly was in her bedroom in the Peshwar Palace, standing on a footstool while Natasha and Salila busied themselves with wrapping her in a sari of scarlet silk.

Under the sari, Olly wore a tight-fitting, short-sleeved shirt, and a narrow silk petticoat. She watched herself in the mirror as the beautiful material was wound around her. The dazzling strip of silk was about fifteen feet long and almost three feet wide. She couldn't quite work out how it could be transformed into a dress, but as Natasha and Salila tucked and pleated it expertly into place — without any buttons or pins or fastenings — it all began to make sense. Finally, Natasha lifted up the one free end of the sari and draped it elegantly over Olly's shoulder.

Olly gazed at the result. "I look amazing!" she breathed in delight.

"Yes, you do," Natasha agreed with a smile.

"How many people did you say this broadcast would be going out to worldwide?" Olly asked.

Natasha grinned. "Oh, only about eighty million — something like that."

Olly couldn't really picture 80 million people all sitting in front of their TV sets to watch her and Josh appear on the news. It didn't really seem real. But it was!

As soon as news of the discovery of the talisman had leaked out, the producers of *Collision Course* had seen the potential for some huge publicity for their movie. And things had moved very quickly after that. Arrangements had been made for a big joint party to announce the end of filming and the astounding discovery of one of the lost Talismans of the Moon.

The party was due to start in about half an hour. Already there were dozens of people downstairs, gathering in the palace ballroom. All day, Olly and Josh had watched the TV vans arriving and lights, cameras, and other equipment being unloaded into the hotel.

"What if my mind goes blank and I can't think of anything to say?" Olly asked in a sudden attack of nerves.

"That won't happen," Natasha replied calmly, looping the final length of her own sari over her shoulder and tucking it into place. "Just relax and imagine you're chatting to your friends."

Olly looked doubtfully at her. "I don't have eighty million friends," she said.

Natasha laughed. "Josh will be with you — and Jonathan and your father. It'll be fine, just you see."

Olly frowned. "I'm not so sure Dad will want to be there," she said. "He hates this kind of thing. He said it was all a 'pointless distraction' taking him away from his proper work of investigating the Elephant of Parvati." She looked at Natasha. "He's really not into wearing a dinner jacket, either. Even if you do manage to drag him to the party, he'll probably turn up wearing a big sweater and a pair of old corduroy pants. You know what he's like!"

"Ethan has all that under control, don't you worry," Natasha assured her. She smiled at Olly. "I'm so proud of the way you and Josh helped him with this whole thing," she said. "He might not have even been here tonight, if it wasn't for Josh. You're both very brave."

Olly gave a quick smile. It was pointless for her to ruin the evening by trying to tell Natasha what had really been going on since their arrival in India. She would never believe that her boyfriend was a scheming rat who only wanted the talisman for himself.

As far as Olly could tell, Ethan was lapping up the media attention. It was he who had coordinated the whole party and the live news broadcast with the producers of *Collision Course*. He had been pulling strings and using all of his considerable influence to make sure everything went with a spectacular bang.

Natasha looked at her watch. "Speaking of Ethan, I'd better go and check that he's ready," she said. She gave Olly a final once-over. "You look gorgeous. And remember, just relax and be yourself." And so saying, she left the room.

Olly gazed thoughtfully after her for a few moments, and then turned to Salila. "But what if being myself includes tripping over the sari and landing flat on my face?" she demanded.

Salila grinned. "I don't think you will do that," she replied.

Olly sighed and climbed down off the foot stool. She looked at herself in the mirror one last time. "OK," she said. "Let's go and make a big entrance!"

The reception area of the hotel was crowded with a throng of people. Olly met Josh at the head of the stairs. He was dressed in a dinner jacket.

"Nice sari," he said, grinning at her.

"Thanks," she said. "You look very suave — very James Bond."

"Ethan organized it," Josh replied. "Ethan organized everything."

"I bet he did," Olly murmured under her breath.

Josh leaned in close. "Don't worry about it," he whispered. "Remember: We were the ones who found the talisman — not Ethan."

Olly looked at him. "Are you nervous at all?" she asked.

Josh looked thoughtful. "I don't think so," he said. He gestured down the long stairway toward the crowds. "All this doesn't seem real, if you know what I mean. It's like it's not really happening. And I certainly can't get my head around the idea of sixty million people watching us on TV. That's totally mind-blowing!"

"Eighty million," Olly corrected him.

"Is that right?" Josh grinned at her. "You know," he said, "somehow, the extra twenty million doesn't bother me at all."

Audrey Beckmann appeared and gave Olly a hug. She was wearing a sari of deep blue silk. Jonathan and Professor Christie were with her. Olly stared at her father in amazement — he was wearing a tuxedo. Although he looked slightly uncomfortable in it, he was smiling and had a look of quiet pride on his face.

Olly turned to see Natasha and Ethan down below, surrounded by a crowd of people. Just then, Ethan swung around and looked up at them. He smiled and waved. Gritting her teeth, Olly waved back.

Ethan made his way to the foot of the stairs and called for silence. "Please welcome our guests of honor," he declared. "Olly and Josh — two intrepid young people who I am proud to call my friends! Olly and Josh, everyone!"

Applause broke out as Olly's grandmother whispered in Olly's ear. "That's your cue," she said. "Down you go."

Olly and Josh looked at each other.

"Come on," Josh said. "Our public awaits!"

Side by side, they began to descend the broad marble staircase.

"I'll trip," Olly whispered. "I haven't had much luck with stairs recently."

"This time, you won't trip," Josh told her.

And Olly found that he was right. As she walked slowly down the stairs with the applause ringing in her ears, her nerves evaporated in the thrill of the moment.

~~~~

The live TV broadcast was due to begin in a few minutes. Olly and Josh were sitting on the steps that overlooked the garden. Once again, the moon was riding high in a clear, starlit sky.

"I could get used to all this media stuff," Olly said. "Just think, in a few minutes, we're going to be in an interview that will be seen all over the world."

"We'll be famous," Josh said softly. "Isn't that a weird thought?"

Olly frowned. "Yes," she said. "Very weird." She grinned. "But still totally amazing!"

"When we've done our part, Jonathan and your dad and Professor Singh are going to be interviewed, too," Josh said. "And so is Ethan, of course."

"I'm not worried about anything he might say," Olly said firmly. "We know the truth, and that's all that matters."

"*And* we beat him again," Josh added.

Olly nodded. "It's about time he realized he's never going to get the better of us." She laughed.

Josh gave her an anxious look. "Don't say that — you might jinx it!"

"It's a pity Mr. Ram wouldn't agree to come," Olly sighed. "We wouldn't have gotten anywhere without him."

"I don't think this is really his kind of thing," Josh replied, looking over his shoulder and in through the open French doors to where the party was in full swing. "I think he's happier up in the hills with his elephants. But we have to mention how much he helped us."

"Of course we do," Olly agreed. "I've just thought of something. Remember what he said — about the seeker having to crack the nutshell to find the kernel within? Do you think that meant I was *supposed* to drop the china elephant in order to find the talisman?"

Josh smiled at her. "As Mr. Ram would say, 'Only the seeker can answer that,'" he replied.

"Just think," Olly said, "if I hadn't dropped it, the Elephant of Parvati might never have been found."

Just then, Salila came running out of the hotel. "The news reporters are ready for you now," she said excitedly. "The broadcast will begin in five minutes."

Olly and Josh stood up and followed her back into the room. A huge plasma screen had been set up at one end, and as they walked through the crowds of people, Olly saw their own faces filling the screen as a camera tracked them.

Olly leaned over to whisper to Josh. "You know something," she said. "We'd better get used to this. If we find any more talismans, I can see us becoming international TV personalities."

Josh nodded. "Maybe Mom was right," he said. "Maybe we can be glamorous celebrities *and* legendary archaeologists, after all!"